David

The Six Macs and the Purple Orb

Austin Macauley Publishers™
London • Cambridge • New York • Sharjah

A CIP catalogue record for this title is available from the British Library.

ISBN 9781398454309 (Paperback)
ISBN 9781398454316 (ePub e-book)

www.austinmacauley.com

First Published 2022
Austin Macauley Publishers Ltd®
1 Canada Square
Canary Wharf
London
E14 5AA

Table of Contents

The Six Macs

Scruffy MacTuffy
Never washes and
wears scruffy clothes

Chaffy MacTaffy
Comes from Wales.

Prancer MacDancer
The coolest one goes to dancing lesson and does skateboard stunts.

Flyer MacHigher.
A whizz on a skateboard.

Maltliquor MacSnigger
Drank something of his dads and ended up in hospital.

Broozer MacDoozer
Likes a punch up.

1. The Tournament

Higher MacFlyer had been awake for most of the night. She was so excited about the skateboard tournament she was entering later that day. Also, it was the first day of her summer holidays. After the tournament, she is going camping with the Six Macs and Chaffy MacTaffy's uncle and aunt. She jumped out of her bed straight into the shower, then put on some new clothes. Her mum had bought her them, especially for the tournament, including a fantastic looking red tartan hat. She took her lucky shamrock badge out of her old tatty hat, then pinned it to her nice new one. Then went straight to the mirror to admire herself, her green and white tee-shirt and blue skirt looked perfect. After breakfast, MacFlyer strapped her skateboard to her back and jumped on her bike. She arrived at the camp where she was meeting the boys earlier than them, so she had some extra time to practice some of her skateboard moves. But first, a quick text to remind her friends from school that she was competing today and to be there to watch her.

She started with the Fakie Beta Flip, which she did perfectly, then a few laser flips and again ten out of ten. Then suddenly she fell over, her knee pads took the full force of the fall, so she was all right. In the corner of her eye, she saw Prancer MacDancer jumping off his bike.

He shouted in a joking voice, "Ha, ha, you're not going to win the tournament like that."

"Typical, you had to catch me the time I fell over. I've been doing some really dodgy moves perfectly. I'll show you."

Then a perfect Fakie Beta Flip was performed right in front of MacDancer eyes. "Wow, I can't do one of those not many people can, you could win this afternoon." Smiled Prancer.

Then MacFlyer heard clapping noises. She turned around and was the rest of the gang who had arrived just after MacDancer. "Hi, guys, thank you," she shouted over to them while waving her slightly dirty hand.

They all stood in a circle, then thrust their arms into the air with clenched fists and then shouted, "The Six Macs."

Scruffy MacTuffy added, "And let the best girl win."

"I think we should go. I don't want to be late." Smiled Flyer.

"We have ages yet and it's only four miles away." Shrugged Chaffy MacTaffy.

"But I want to go now, anything can happen in four miles," demanded Flyer.

So they got onto their bikes and rode off. There was a traffic jam with traffic lights but they managed to wriggle their way to the front. On the side of the road, where a few men in orange high vis jackets wielding petrol-driven smoky chainsaws. Three of the men were cutting down a great big oak tree. They were right up at the top sawing off small branches which were crashing to the ground – which was the reason for the traffic lights just in case a branch fell on top of a car.

It didn't take long to get there and they were only two hours early. Flyer gave Broozer MacDoozer her phone.

"Can you please take a video of me so that I can show my mum and da?"

"Sure." Smiled Broozer.

Then Flyer headed straight into the park, disappearing into a mass of competitors. All practising their twists and jumps and all the other things you do on a skateboard. Prancer MacDancer was also competing. He was in the special gymnastic group. They did stunts on skateboards like jumping over stacks of logs and doing somersaults. There was also a section in the competition where he had to jump from a high wall over to other, then over to an even higher wall while doing a double somersault. It was a very dangerous move, one slip could mean ending up in hospital. It was the only part when a skateboard was not needed. He had been practising for a long time at his school with his favourite teacher. He gave his phone to Maltliquor while the others sat in a corner. Maltliquer MacSnigger gets a few cans of Coca-Cola out of his rucksack and hands them around to his friends.

"Cheers, here's to Flyer and Prancer." As he raises his coke can into the air, the others crash their cans against his.

Two hours passed really quickly, they heard Prancer MacDancer name called out. So, they rushed to the fence all watching in anticipation. Prancer whizzed past them, then he did his favourite manoeuvre by jumping high into the air, followed by a double somersault. Everybody roared. He looked really cool in his white designer tee-shirt and his red tartan kilt which swished with every move. The four Macs noticed he was the only one wearing black jeans under his kilt.

"Wow, he's fantastic, what a move," shouted Broozer.

Over by the gymnastic section they could see him jumping here and jumping there with some very high somersaults, everybody was clapping.

Prancer was very nervous; he didn't like performing in front of loads of people. Also, he had also been worried about slipping up because he had hurt his ankle jumping over a fence on the way to school a couple of weeks back. "Fantastic." Cried Scruffy.

He was called Scruffy because he was. He was the only one who wore short trousers and he seemed to wear the same pair for weeks. He always turned up in a dirty tee-shirt, it's if his mum doesn't have a washing machine.

Then they heard MacFlyers name called out. There she was in all her new clothes looking quite proud with her new hat on. First, she did a few laser flips, then a Gazelle Flip, then a Hard Flip followed by an amazing Fakie Beta Flip. The crowd gave out a loud roar, it was a perfect ten.

MacFlyer had a smile on her face as wide as a crocodile as a gold medal was pinned onto her tee-shirt. Prancer was next to receive his.

"Oh, yes, a double whammy," roared Broozer, who always likes to wear a blue tee-shirt and blue jeans.

Prancer promised himself that he is going to keep his gold medal on for the whole holiday. Prancer was the first to congratulate Flyer.

"You're almost as good as me," joked Prancer.

"I have never seen anyone as good as you, you were the best." Beamed Flyer.

"We have to get back home, my uncle is picking us in his minibus later this afternoon," said Chaffy MacTaffy, who likes to be different by wearing a green and white tartan scarf because he's from Wales, which matches his green trousers. He always wears a yellow tee-shirt, he owns thirty-one of them, all in different shades. He tells everybody he just loves yellow.

"How exciting, I have never been camping with you lot before. I did go camping with my friends from school a couple of years ago and ended up getting in trouble." Grinned Maltliquor MacSnigger.

While cycling home they noticed that the traffic light had gone, so was the beautiful old oak tree. All that was left was a few twigs and a pile of sawdust. "Dad said that the council is widening the road, so even more cars can use this road." Sighed Broozer MacDoozer. They all arrived home safely. After putting their bikes away, they put the final bits and pieces into their rucksacks.

2. The Trip

Maltliquor MacSnigger stuffed his rucksack with as many Coca-Cola cans that he could get in, making it very heavy and lumpy. His mum has bought him a new sleeping bag because his old one had a few holes in and she was worried about red ants getting in and biting his feet. Flyer MacHigher ran into her house to show her mum and da her gold medal and the video on her phone of her moves.

Chaffy MacTaffy's uncle drove around to each one of their houses to pick them up.

Chaffy's uncle stood up and shouted, "Hi, my name is Bruce, what are your names?" Each one, in turn, told Bruce their names. They gave him their real names, not their Mac names, they were secret. It was a three-hour road trip, so they all got their phones out to text friends.

"We're here," shouted Bruce.

Chaffy's aunt was waiting in the drive, she didn't look very friendly. "My name is Bonnie." She looked at Bruce then said, "Oow, you are looking a bit pale. Are you feeling unwell?"

“I think I’m coming down with a bad cold.” Sniffled Bruce.

All the macs looked at each other, all thinking that their camping trip could be called off.

Bonnie said to Bruce, “I think the only place you’re going is to a bed.”

She then piped loudly, “I think you six can go by yourselves. But instead of going up into the mountains you can camp in a wood that we own, which is just over that hill.” Pointing to a hill about five hundred metres away. She continued, “There is a clearing in the centre where you can light a fire and there’s a stream running through where you can fish. It’s all worked out then. There you go, everything is just fine, because really I’m not too keen on camping myself, I like my own bed.” She continued talking not one of the Six Macs could get a word in.

“In fact, I will drive you there right now. We have a solar-powered fridge full of food, including some really delicious bacon and sausage that came from our organic butchers not far from here.”

“I like bacon,” Broozer whispered into Flyer’s ear.

Bonnie kept talking, “I have packed pots, pans and lots of pop and you can cook, can’t you?” Prancer was just about to answer but Bonnie continued,

“Now you all have waterproofs, don’t you? And wellies in case it rains and you know how to put up your tents, don't you? Come with me and help me put the fridge in the van."

"Oww, ow, this fridge is really heavy, grab a corner, Prancer," complained Chaffy.

"Wow," Broozer MacDoozer whispered to Flyer.

"I think she wants to get rid of us."

"I'm going to run it, I want to practice for the Edinburgh marathon. In fact, I might even beat you." Laughed Prancer.

He then put on a quite fancy pair of running shoes.

"You better be quick. I want to explain a few things once we get into the woods. I have to get back here as soon as possible. We have a delivery of tree saplings." Stressed Bonie.

Before they knew it, they were in the van, then it seemed just a few seconds before they were standing in the woods with all their gear. None of them still had not spoken a word because Bonnie had been talking all the way from the house, she continued, "Now you know where are house is, it's just over that hill, so were not that far away if you get into trouble. Oh, before I go just over there behind those bushes." Bonnie pointed to a holly bush.

"There are about fifty of the rarest orchids in Scotland. They're protected so don't go over near them. Well, maybe we should take a look at them now, so you know where they are, come with me." As she strutted towards a prickly mass of holly bushes. They all walked around to the other side of the bushes peering in wonder.

"There you are, aren't they delicate white flowers beautiful? There called Young's Helleborine." Beamed Bonnie. "Oh, dear, is that the time I will see you in a week then." As she climbed into the minibus, in seconds she was gone.

3. The Discovery

They were all in a state of shock, one minute they were supposed to be camping with Bruce and Bonnie in the mountains and the next minute they were standing in the woods all by themselves. At that second Prancer came puffing through the trees.

"Wow, that was further than I expected, did I miss anything?" Puffed Prancer.

"Take a look at what we are sharing the woods with, close your eyes," Flyer said as she grabbed Prancer's hand leading him to the other side of the holly bushes.

"You can open your eyes now," suggested Flyer. "Aren't they beautiful? They're the rarest orchids in Scotland, Chaffy's aunt showed them to us. They're called Young's Helleborine they're protected. We are so lucky to have seen them but even luckier to be camping in the same wood as them." Smiled Flyer.

Prancer suddenly boomed out, "Yer, they're beautiful but there's something even more absolutely fantastic. We get to do what we want to do for a whole week with no adults. I don't want to sound horrible

Chaffy, but I am not sure if I could have put up with your aunt talking all the time."

"Yes, I sort of know what you mean. She could have driven us all mad." Sneered Chaffy. He then added, "I have only met my aunt and uncle once with my mum and dad, they used to live in America."

"Let's put up our tents in a circle, then we can have the fire in the middle," suggested Prancer.

"Yer, this is going to be the best holiday we have ever had. I don't like climbing hills, so we can just chill-lax and drink lots of Cocoa Cola." Beamed Maltliquor MacSnigger. He likes wearing blue jeans all of the time and always turns up with a different coloured tee-shirt that clash with his bright orange glasses.

Prancer's tent was bright blue with two white crosses on each side that looked like the Scottish flag. All the other tents were yellow except flyers, which was tartan, she thought it was really cool and so did the others.

After putting up their tents, they gathered in a circle, then put their arms in the air with clenched fists and shouted, "The Six Macs."

Then the gang thought they would explore the wood and look for some wood for the fire. "Bonnie has left us a saw, so we can cut a small tree down," said Scruffy MacTuffy.

"No," shouted Flyer. "Let's just look for old fallen branches. I don't like chopping down trees, I don't even like cutting branches off trees, they're living things you know"

Suddenly the quietness of the wood broke with the sound of loud voices and noises of sticks bashing on tree trunks.

"Get down," shouted Scruffy MacTuffy.

They all dived into some bracken which hid a small gorse bush, Chaffy was the one who ended up landing on top of it.

"Ow, ow, ow, owch," he screamed loudly. "SSSSSS HHHHHHHHHHH," they all said. Luckily, nobody else heard him.

"Owwwww," Chaffy whispered as he pulled a few gorse prickles out of his trousers. Suddenly they spotted four lads appear out of some bushes, who looked much older than them. They were messing around in the woods about ten metres away from them. Near a few white pitched tents, the Six Macs kept still.

"I think we should go and say hello and if they're not friendly I will punch one of them," whispered Broozer.

"No, you're always after a punch up, where on holiday let's just watch, they'll go back to their tents soon." Pleaded Prancer.

As they watched, they saw them lift up a heavy slab of rock then put something under it. The Six Macs could hear them taking.

"It could be a glow-worm."

"No, don't be silly, a glow-worm is a beetle."

"It's not a beetle, it's a worm that's why it's called a glow-worm."

"I know it's a beetle. I will prove it when we get home."

"Well, this isn't a beetle or a worm. It looks very much like a snail."

One of them SLAMMED the slab back down on the ground, which looked really heavy. Then all four of them started to walk in the direction of the small village where Bruce and Bonnie live. They waited for about ten minutes just in case the boys came back, then they went over to the slab.

"Cccccome on, give me a hand," stammered Chaffy MacTaffy.

"We shouldn't really lift it up, it's not ours to lift," argued Prancer.

"It's not theirs, it's a slab of rock in a wood," added Broozer.

Broozer stepped forward and gave Chaffy a hand. As they lifted it up, there was a hole underneath it. To their amazement, the hole was lit by a purple light. At the bottom, about a metre down was a round ball of purple light. There was also an old rusty watch, a muddy red vase and a bicycle bell.

"What is it?" asked Flyer.

"I don't know," shrugged Prancer.

"How amazing, it's a wee snail with a purple light in its shell." Smiled Chaffy.

"Oooow, it's spooky, it's a purple snail ghost." Teased Scruffy.

"I've never seen anything like it but I did read about a type of snail that you only find deep in the deepest ocean," said Prancer.

"Yer, but were in a wood, how do you explain that?" Probed Broozer.

"Let's pick it up," suggested Flyer.

She stretched down and grabbed it, her face lit up with glee as it slimmed across her hand.

Prancer was right, it certainly was a snail. It had lots of different shades of purple light shining through its pale white opalescent large round shell. All six looked with amazement. Looking down into the hole they noticed that it was very dry and there was no vegetation for the snail to eat.

"I think we should take it and give it something to eat, do we all agree?" asked Flyer. They all agreed, then put the slab back on top of the hole, Flyer carefully held the purple snail in her hand.

As they started walking back to their camp, the purple snail started to get brighter which they thought was odd. Flyer had to rush back because she had left her new hat next to the hole, she noticed that the purple snail had got dimmer. When she got back to the boys, it had gone brighter again. She told the boys but they weren't that interested. All they could think about was food.

Arriving back at camp, they noticed that one of them had left the fridge door open. All five Macs looked at Maltliquor, then stared at the open fridge. They could tell it was Maltliquor because he had his guilty face on.

It looked like a fox had helped itself to a few rashers of bacon, which they were looking forward to eating for breakfast.

"Oh, Maltliquor, look what you have done, you're not having any bacon for your breakfast for the rest of the week," grunted Broozer.

Flyer put the purple snail carefully in a Tupperware plastic box which had some salad leaves in it. She took most of them out leaving a few for the purple snail to eat and then pierced the lid with several breathing holes.

It was late, so they lit a fire and cooked seventeen of the sausages, then heated some beans. As a joke, Prancer gave Maltliquor only two sausages instead of three.

"Hey, where's my other sausage?" complained Maltliquor.

"It's in the fox," teased Prancer.

Maltliquor as quick as a flash, wielding his fork, launched himself towards Prancer's plate. With precision, he speared one of Prancer sausages, then ran off into the woods. Prancer jumped up and then took chase.

"Oy, give me back my sausage," he shouted.

He eventually caught up with Maltliquor wrestling him to the ground, only to find that Maltliquor had already eaten it. Prancer helped Maltquor up.

"Are you all right?" he asked.

"Yes, I'm fine," answered Maltliquor.

"I'm going to get you back for that one." Laughed Prancer MacDancer.

Prancer had brought his guitars to play and sing a few songs around the campfire but they were all too tired and just wanted to go to sleep. Maltliquor has brought a torch that stays on all night with a dim light because he was not too keen of the dark, especially in a tent in the middle of a wood all by himself.

"Hey, Maltliquor, are you scared of the dark?" shouted Broozer, so that everyone could hear. Maltliquor had to make a story up really quick.

"NO, I JUST LIKE TO SEE WHAT THE TIME IS IF I WAKE WHEN IT'S DARK," he shouted back even louder.

Flyer said that she would look after the snail which gave her tent a purple glow.

4. Jack of the Woods

They all fell asleep very quickly. During the night Flyer started a have a very strange dream. Her dream sent her floating through the wood with the purple snail. Next to her was a green woman made of wood, leaves and moss, all tangled up in a mishmash. She was holding her hand which was warm and she was smiling. Then in her dream Flyer was no longer in the wood, instead she was in a hollow underground cavern with lots of roots hanging from the ceiling. The strange green woman started to talk to her in a young girl's voice, "My name is Jack, Jack of the woods. In a wood far from here there is a great underground Lake of Life. My Purple Orbs have two very important purposes. Firstly, they feed on the sediment, which gets washed in from thousands of underwater streams, keeping my Lake of Life as pure as white crystal."

"Their second purpose is that on nights of a full moon, all my Purples Orbs leave their deep underground lake to congregate in an opening on the surface, where the bright moon shines brightest. They absorb energy from the moon into their shells. Over the period between full moons my Purple Orbs transfer their energy into The Lake of Life, which feeds all trees and plants helping them to flourish and live long lives."

"All of my Purple Orbs have to be present or I will start to fade," whispers Jack.

"Why do you say my trees and my plants and my Purple Orbs?" asked Flyer.

"I am Jack, Jack of the woods. I am the spirit, the spirit of all trees. I look after everything, everything that grows, everything that is green," answered Jack as she breezed past Flyer. She continued, "My Lake of Life is the life force for all my trees and plants. Their roots are entwined joining all plants and trees together from all over this land. For millions of years there has been the same number of Purple Orbs. Before a Purple orb dies it lays one egg, which replaces the old dead one, keeping my great underground lake stable. Water rained down with force coursing a great underground flood. Sweeping away some of my Purple Orbs up through a hole that your mankind dug with giant mechanical monsters. My lost Purple Orbs then slithered into my wood. My Purple Orbs can only live out of my Lake of Life for five days.

"Two days have passed since our great flood. They must be found before they die and before this summer's moon. My Purple Orbs must be taken back to the great Lake of Life. I cannot take my Purple Orbs back because I am a spirit, a spirit of the woods. The Purple Orb, that you have, will go brighter if you are going the right way. It must be kept in water or else it will dry up and die. If it dies, you must keep the egg, it hatches safe. It is very, very small yellow pearl of light that glows extremely brightly. All Purple Orbs have to be present under the bright moon if not, trees will start to die with diseases. Dutch Elm trees are still dying from the time of the last great flood when many Purple Orbs were lost for many moons. If the great Lake of Life is ever destroyed, all trees and plants from this land will die and I will fade forever, fade forever, fade forever, forever, forever, ever, ever, ever," Jack whispered quieter and quieter until her voice could be heard no more.

The next morning everybody woke up, a warm sun was shining through their tents, which made it hot inside, so they couldn't get out into the cool fresh air fast enough. After getting dressed, they all brushed their teeth except for Scruffy who pretended to. Scruffy lit a fire which smoked at first from damp wood.

Then Prancer suddenly said, "Where's Flyer?"

They all looked at each other, they hadn't noticed Flyer's absence.

Scruffy shouted outside her tent, "FLYER, ARE YOU IN THERE?"

There was no answer, he took a look inside her tent, there was no sign of her, just an empty sleeping bag.

"Where can she be?" quizzed Prancer. "Mmmaybe the snail ate hhher." Laughed Chaffy.

"Yer, maybe it was a monster in disguise, and it ate her," shrieked Maltliquor.

"Don't be silly," snapped Prancer. He hated the thought of Flyer being eaten by a giant snail.

Meanwhile, Flyer had woken up. For a split second she was sure she was tucked in her sleeping bag inside her tent. Then,

"ARRRRRRR, where am I? HEEEEELP," she shouted really loud in shock.

She looked around, she found herself on a bed of straw inside an underground cavern. *What, What am I doing here? Could I have slept walked, then fallen down this hole?* she thought to herself.

"HEEEEEEEELLLLLP," she whaled.

She was so, so frightened but how strange, it was very strange. She was down underground but it wasn't dark. There was a hole at the top of her that brought in bright rays from a warm morning sun, which shone down on to her head. But there was another source of light. As she looked deeper down into the winding tunnel, she could see tiny lights that lit the eerie wet extending hole of scariness, which gave her a real spooky feeling making her climb up, though the whole as fast as she could.

Once out, she looked back and saw the Tupperware box.

Oh, no, I've left the purple snail down the hole, she thought. She laid down flat on some wet slightly muddy grass, so she could reach down to pick it up.

She started to remember the dream, then realised that it may have been true because it felt so real. Flyer could remember every word that the strange little woman told her. Her new clothes were covered in mud which made her feel miffed. As she made her way back to camp, she waded through tuffs of ferns which were soaked with dew, making her legs cold and wet. At first, she thought she was lost but then saw the tents of the four lads, which she sneaked past. She noticed that they weren't anywhere to be seen and thought that probably they had not spent the night camping there.

She then saw the slab of rock, which wasn't far from camp. Broozer was the first to spot Flyer coming out from the wood. He shouted, "Hey, Flyer, where have you been?"

The others stopped what they were doing, then rusher over to Flyer.

"We were getting worried about you, did you get up early and go for a walk?" asked Prancer.

"NO, I didn't," she sniffled.

She cupped her hands then started to cry.

"You're shaking," cried Scruffy.

"Sit here by the fire," Maltliquor said in a soft voice.

"Here, drink this hot tea." Sighed Prancer.

"I feel better now, thank you." Smiles Flyer.

All of them just wanted to know where she has been and what happened to her.

"Was it those boys we saw yesterday? Did they attack you? I'm goin' to look for them and punch them in the nose," roared Broozer.

"No." Fretted Flyer. "I don't know where to start, one minute I was asleep in my tent. Then I had a really strange dream. It's as if it was real but it wasn't. But it must have been. No, I don't know, there was this old, no, young woman or girl, all dressed in green. She had a strange costume on or did she? It was covered with sticks and leaves and moss and, ow, I don't know. She said her name was Jack, Jack of the wood."

Chaffy interrupted, "The Green Man, we learned about that subject at school. The green man or Jack of the wood is a tree spirit who was worshipped by the old English Pagans hundreds of years ago."

"Yer, I remember learning about that subject in my Primary school," declared Prancer.

"But she wasn't a man, she was a woman or a girl." stressed Flyer.

"Maybe all the history books have got it wrong, maybe everybody presumed the Green Man was a man because her name is Jack. If you know what I mean," explained Chaffy.

"Yer, really weird," added Broozer.

"So what hhhhappened next?" asked Chaffy.

"She spoke to me in my dream, she said something like, ow, I'm not sure. She called our snail a Purple Orb, then she said there was a great flood. And something about a Lake of Life and we must rescue our snail. Then take it back to the lake or something like that, or else all trees will die. And something about men digging, Ow, I'm not sure," Flyer said in a confused manner as she scratched her head.

"Ow, yes, and something about the Orb which will go brighter if we are going the right way. Ahh, yes, and there was a big flood and loads of Purple Orbs were washed away into the wood. And we have to find them, we only have five days or trees will die. Yes, yes, I remember no. If the lake is destroyed, all trees and everything will die. Then I found myself underground very muddy with the purple snail and now I'm here," explained Flyer, who was still quivering.

"Wwwwwow-yowee," stammered Chaffy.

"From now on, we should call our purple snail the Purple Orb out of respect," demanded Flyer.

5. The Four Lads

"Right, we need a plan. I'm goin' for it, we have nothing else to do. Who's with me?" asked Flyer.

They all agreed, then put their arms in the air with clenched fists, then shouted, "The Six Macs."

"For starters, we have to hide the fridge. Or else those boys will know that we camped here and will probably guess that we stole their snail, any ideas?" asked Prancer.

"I reckon we should dig a hole for it. Then if we lay it on its side, we could cover it with bracken," suggested Maltliquor, who had just started on his second can of coke.

"Great! That sounds good to me. You can start digging while the rest of us take down our tents and bury the embers from the fire if that is OK?" asked Prancer.

"But first, we should take as much food as we can carry out of the fridge." Sniffled Scruffy.

"And all the pop," added Maltliquor, who wished he had not suggested digging a hole. He hates digging, it's too much like hard work. He would prefer to sit and text friends while drinking coke and eating sweets. Also, the spade that they had brought with them was too small to dig a large hole. He thought, *It's going to take me hours.* A bright idea sprung into his head with the fridge being out of sight of the others. He thought if he ties the spare rope he had brought for his tent around it, he could throw the other end over a high branch, then pull the fridge high into the air. It was so much easier which made him quite proud of his idea but he decided not to tell the others.

"All done," he shouted.

"That was quick. You must be fitter than you look," joked Broozer.

"We're all finished. Here's your tent. We took it down for you," said Chaffy.

The Purple Orb seemed to shine brighter if they walked east according to Prancer's compass. Maltliquer looked back, the only thing that caught his eye was a fridge hanging in the trees. It seemed really high up in the tree at the time but now that they are further away, it was really obvious. It stuck out like a sore thumb. He rushed up to the front of the Mac's setting a faster pace, hoping that none of them turned around to see the fridge hanging in the trees.

After walking for about half a mile, the sun came out again making it a fairly hot day, the perfect holiday weather. Flyer passed around the sun cream before texting a friend about her dream. "It's a really beautiful day but last night I had a really weird dream, last night I…"

Meanwhile, back in Bonnies wood, the older lads returned. Their names are David, Frank, Greg and Trevor, all of them came from Petersfield in Hampshire. Apart from Greg, who was from Glasgow, he has relatives down in the village, Trevor, David and Frank stay with Greg's relatives each year. They have done since they all met on a holiday in Norfolk when they were six years old. It's quite amazing that they still get on as they all have totally different personalities. All four of them are quite laid back, so they enjoy meeting each year. Trevor is always listening to music with his earphones on, he is really into blues music. David likes to do all the cooking to the relief of the others. Frank likes to sketch and make a model out of anything he can find and Greg likes to build things out of wood but tends to spend most of his time texting.

They headed straight to their secret hiding place but then noticed that the stone had moved. David quickly lifted it up. He was the strongest one out of them all. His dad is a tree surgeon and he tends to help him at weekends for extra pocket money. To their disappointment, their glowing snail had gone.

Trevor said, "Oh, well, it must have escaped. It was only a snail. I think we should camp tonight next to the river, today is going to be hot, so we should take our kayak with us." He stood up, then turned around and the first thing he saw was a fridge hanging in the trees. "What's that in the trees?" he shouted.

"It looks like a fridge. How strange, it looks like a piece of art," blurted Frank. "It's typical you can't go anywhere without seeing rubbish, even in the middle of the countryside, I hate fly tippers." Groaned David.

They went over to the tree where the fridge was hanging from. Trevor grabbed the rope before lowering it down to the ground. Inside, there wasn't much apart from about twenty sausages hidden right at the back behind a few pork chops. Greg and Trevor are vegetarians. Frank said, "Ooww, I like sausages but I'm not too keen on pork chops." As he throws each one into various parts of the wood.

He then wraps the sausages into a plastic bag before putting them into his bag.

The lads noticed that some bracken had been trampled down which had made a path through the wood towards the river.

"That's odd, each year we never see anyone in this wood. This year there's a hanging fridge with food in it up in the trees and it looks to me that someone had a fire here last night. I wonder who they are?" asked Frank.

"I think I know who they are. My nanna lives next to an American lady, who told her that her nephew was coming to stay for a week. It could be him with his friends," answered Greg. "Let's follow the flattened bracken to see who is on the end of it. It's in the same direction that we're going," suggested David.

6. Heading for the Wood

The Six Macs decided to stop for a rest, Maltliquor cracked open another can. Flyer got on her phone, the other four started messing around by trying to give each other dead legs. "You're acting like small children, how old are you?" Flyer asked.

"It's payback time, Maltliquor MacSnigger. I'll teach you to steal a sausage from me." Chortled Prancer as he gave Maltliquor a punch to his upper leg.

"Oooow, ow, ow, that hurt." Laughed Maltliquor.

Chaffy checked the Purple Orb, it was rather dull, so he poured more water into the box.

"Right, then let's go," shouted Flyer.

They noticed the Orb was starting to shine brighter again through the plastic box. Also, ahead of them the wood seemed to be coming to an end.

"What now? Where do we go from here?" asked Chaffy.

They turned to walk north but the Orb went very dull. Then they turned to walk south, the Orb went dull again.

"So we keep going east then," instructed Flyer.

For some mad reason, Broozer decided to run as fast as he could across the field ahead of the others. He thought he was running across just a grassy field but he was wrong. There was a small pond in the middle and he ran straight into it right up to his waist. “Have you decided to go for a swim?” Teased Scruffy.

One mad moment meant he was now soaking, his trousers, his boots, and the bottom of his rucksack where all dripping wet and now he’s cold and smells like a stinky pond. “Was it worth the run?” Joked Maltliquor. “I suppose not but I just fancied a run.” Grunted Broozer.

Broozer was just starting to dry out but he still stunk of a smelly pond. All of them noticed that the path was starting to go downhill, it was getting quite steep. Maltliquor suddenly slipped over, which woke him up from a daydream about stopping and drinking a can of coke.

“Ow, that hurt.” He grunted as he rubbed his butt.

“Is that water I can hear?” shouted Chaffy.

“Yes, it sounds like a raging torrent,” cried Maltliquor.

They were still going down the hill when suddenly Prancer stopped abruptly before leaning back against the others.

“Wow, that was a close one, one more step and I would have fallen off this rock straight into that raging torrent.”

“Wow, it’s amazing, it’s so noisy,” shouted Flyer.

“So how are we going to cross this?” screamed Maltliquor.

“I don’t know,” shouted Prancer.

“I think we should try to look for a less lively part of the river, maybe by going a bit further downstream,” wailed Broozer.

“Good idea because you know I can’t swim,” shouted Maltliquor.

They went up the path for a while, then found a path that runs along-side the river behind some rocks.

“Watch out for the bees nest,” Flyer MacHigher shouted as she jumped over a log that was in the middle of the path. They all jumped over the log.

After about an eighth a mile they decided to take another look at the river. As they approach it The Six Macs noticed that it was still raging.

“We’re never going to get across that.” Moaned Maltliquor.

They sat looking at the river Maltliquor and opened a can of coke.

“Maltliquor, you’re going to get fat, then explode with gas.” Joked Broozer.

“Where’s Prancer gone?” shouted Scruffy. Who had not said much for a while because he had a toothache, probably from eating too many of his dad’s cakes from his baker’s shop.

“He’s gone to look for a way across.” Coughed Flyer who had just breathed in a mosquito. There seemed to be a lot of them, occasionally they would hear a buzzing in their ears.

Prancer came running back jumping from rock to rock.

"I've found a way to the side. There's a large tree just around the corner that has fallen across the river, Prancer," shouted Prancer.

"I don't like the sound of that," screamed Maltliquor.

They all put their rucksacks back on to their backs. Maltliquor's rucksack was still a lot heavier from loads of coke cans. As they jumped from rock to rock they noticed that the Purple Orb had gone dull. It was because they were not going the right way.

"Here it is," announced Prancer.

"That's easy," shouted Broozer as he jumped onto the fallen tree.

He sat down on it with one leg on each side. He edged his way slowly all the way across to the other side.

"Yippeeee, made it, come on, it's easy." Celebrated Broozer as he jumped up and down like a bit of a twit.

"Who's next?" he shouted.

Prancer followed, Maltliquor went quiet but then to everybody's amazement he started to edge his way across. He was a bit slower than the other two but soon he was on the other side followed by Chaffy and Scruffy. Lastly was Flyer. She had an extra bag with the Purple Orb in, so found the crossing a little more difficult.

Broozer shouted over to Flyer, "Throw the bag over, I'll catch it."

"No, no, I'm OK," screamed Flyer.

She was only halfway across when her hand slipped dropping the bag with the Orb into the water.

She let out a piercing scream, "SCCCCCC REEEAM."

All the others looked with disbelief. As they watched, the bright yellow bag disappear into the raging river of white and black splashing water. Prancer had no time to think. He just jumped in followed by Broozer, who were both really strong swimmers. It all happened so quick, only seconds passed before both of them had disappeared into the distance.

Broozer shouted to Prancer, "Can you see it?"

"Yes, it's over there."

The torrent was tossing them around like a pair of jeans in a washing machine.

"Yes, there it is," screamed Broozer as he stretches out his arm grabbing the bag. "Got it, I have got it, yay, yay. I have got it." He gurgled out loud. They both managed to crawl onto a rock then crawl up the bank.

Broozer suddenly gave a large yowl. "Owwwwwww, look at my leg, I must have bashed it on a rock."

"Oww, that looks sore." Sniffled Prancer.

Broozer had a large gash, just above his knee which was bleeding quite badly. "Let's get back to the others. Chaffy has a medical bag," said Prancer.

Broozer put a brave face on, then they made their way back to the others.

"Oww, that looks bad." Signed Flyer.

Chaffy took out his medical bag, he belongs to St John's ambulance. He meets up with them each week and learns about how to medically heal people, he wants to be a doctor when he leaves school.

"Here, put your leg just here, I hhhave just the right size bbbbandage but first this might hhhurt," stammers Chaffy as he pours TCP over the wound.

He was a little nervous because he doesn't really like the sight of blood. As they walk nearer the path, the Purple Orb started to shine brighter.

It was getting late so Chaffy suggested they set up camp.

"I can see another wood over there, probably about a mile away. I think we should camp there. We will also be able to collect some old wood for a fire," Voiced Flyer.

So they continued walking. When they got to the wood they put up the tents, then lit a fire. Broozer and Prancer put their trousers and boots next to the fire to dry, then they cooked supper.

"I think we should eat the chicken tonight before it goes off," suggested Maltliquor. Prancer got out his guitar.

"He's rather good." yawned Flyer.

The Macs really enjoyed singing the choruses. As it got dark they decided to go to sleep, it had been a tiring day. Scruffy dampen down the fire. One at a time they climb into their tents.

“Night, night, I hope I don’t end up down a hole again tonight,” shouted Flyer.

7. Jack's Return

Later that night Jack of the wood visited Chaffy McTaffy in his dream. "Chaffy, Chaffy," whispered Jack. "You only have two days left, you must return, my Purple Orb. You only have two days, only two days to find all of my lost Purple Orbs. You are now in my wood, in my sacred wood, you have to find my Lake of Life, where my Purple Orbs live. Don't forget, Chaffy, you only have two days left, only two days. You must visit my wise old oak tree – he is 500 years old and he is the biggest and oldest tree in my wood. Hug him and close your eyes, he will bring you joy, he is my friend. You must stop those digging monsters or all will be lost – I will fade, I will fade, fade, you must help, you must help me," she whispered.

Chaffy suddenly woke up. He was cold and soaking wet and more frightening, it was pitch black. He could feel slippery cold walls all around him, his boots were stuck in sticky wet mud underfoot. He was frozen with fear, he couldn't even speak, his bottom lip was starting to quiver. *I must be dead, I must be,* he thought.

Suddenly he saw a mass of tiny lights that lit up the cavern as bright as it was day. Every tree root was alight with lots of tiny lights, also there were thousands of glow-worms that helped illuminate the large cavern in green.

He reluctantly touched one of the lights on a root, which gave him an almighty electric shock that threw him to the opposite side of the cavern. Giving him the fright of his life.

He let out a curdling stammered scream, "HHHHHH EEEEELPPPPP." It was so loud that it woke up the other five Macs.

"That sounded like Chaffy," shouted Prancer from inside his tent.

"It sounded like his voice came from underneath us," screamed Maltliquor. As his legs shook with fright.

They all jumped out of their sleeping bags,

"What's the time?" asked Broozer.

"Half-past seven in the morning." Yawned Scruffy, who still had not washed since leaving home.

"HHHHHHHEEEEEELLLLPPPP."

"That is Chaffy's voice and it, is coming from underneath us," shrieked Maltliquor.

Prancer shouted, "Chaffy, where are you?"

"I'm nnnot sssure, I think I'm underggggggground," he answered.

"Can you get out? Is it dark? Did you see the green woman? What did she say? Are you all right?" asked Flyer, all in one breathe.

"It's not dark, it's strange. All the tree roots are lit up and there's loads of glow-worms. There's a smmmmalll sssqueezable hole ddown tttthe end wwwhich II aaam gggoing to try to get through."

"Keep shouting so that we know where you are," screamed Flyer.

"I'm through but only just, it was so muddy down there and the lit tunnel looked like it went on for miles," shouted Chaffy very loudly.

The other five Macs made their way towards Chaffy. Then there in front of them was Chaffy holding another Purple Orb. He pointed to a dark hole which he had just climbed out of.

"As soon as I surfaced, the root lights went out, it's as if the trees are alive and they knew I was down there. It was really weird I have never seen anything like it." Trembled Chaffy who was still in shock. "You see that's why we should respect trees, they are living just like us. Just because they can't talk doesn't mean that they're not intelligent." Smiled Flyer.

"Look, what I found down there." As he held out his hand. "It's another Purple Orb. Jack said there are quite a few lost ones dotted around his wood. Quickly put this one with your one flyer." Insisted Chaffy.

When Chaffy finally got his voice back from fear, he told the others that one minute he was fast asleep, then the next he was in a horrible dark place. "It seemed like a dream but I soon realised that it was real. Jack of the wood was talking to me and it was very, very dark. Jack said that this is her wood and we only have two days left to find the other Purple Orbs. She kept saying only two days, only two days explained Chaffy."

"Flyer, you told us that we had five days," queried Broozer.

"Maybe I got it wrong, I was so confused," replied Flyer.

"That doesn't give us much time," Prancer said in a worried voice.

"There was one thing that was really strange while I was down there, all the tree roots lit up. I had a strange feeling that the ttttrees were looking after me as if ttttthey were alive or as if they had ffffffeelings but I think they don't like anyone touching their roots because I touched one of the lights and got a nasty electric shock," stammered Chaffy, who was still feeding a bit shaken.

"She also said we have to find the big old oak tree, she said we have to hug it and close our eyes."

"It sounds a bit weird to me." Shuddered Maltliquor.

Flyer was looking on her phone. She had remembered that at school one of her teachers were talking about some research that had come from Germany. About someone, who looks after trees, who has written a book about his thoughts on trees. Her phone reception wasn't really much good but she just managed to find it.

"Hey, guys, have a look at this." Invited Flyer.

(A revolution has been taking place in the scientific understanding of trees. The latest scientific studies, conducted at well-respected universities in Germany and around the world confirm what he has long suspected from close observation in this forest. Trees are far more alert, social, sophisticated—and even intelligent—than we thought).

"What does that mean, sophisticated? Intelligent?" asked Maltliquor.

"You see I was right." Smiled Flyer.

8. Creepy Hole

"We should light a fire to cook breakfast, then climb down into the hole to see if the orb snail shines brighter," suggested Prancer.

"Yer, let's go for it, we'll save the trees," shouted flyer while holding up her arm with a clenched fist.

The other followed and they shouted, "The Six Macs."

"Who's cooking breakfast this morning? How about you, Broozer? You never cook." Suggested Scruffy.

Broozer never cooks because he can't, he tends to burn everything.

"OK, if you want a burnt breakfast, I will," grunted Broozer.

He relented, then started to cook under the watchful eye of all of them.

"It's time to take the sausages off now." Suggested Flyer.

"It's time to take the bacon off now." Suggested Prancer. Then he cooked almost the perfect eggs.

"YUM, that was good, you can cook again." Thanked Maltliquor.

Broozer felt slightly proud but deep down he knew the other helped quite a lot. They wiped their plates with some wet kitchen towel as they sat drinking a cup of tea to wash down breakfast. They noticed that a wind had picked up. Broozed noticed a strange noise that echoed through the wood. As the wind blew, it rustled leaves and whistling through branches, which made a sound something like a heartbeat. As if the wood was alive.

"Can you hear that beating noise?" asked Broozer.

"No," answered Prancer. The other listened but could hear nothing.

"Maybe it's Jack's heartbeat," whispered Broozer.

After drinking their tea, they took five minutes to text but their signals weren't very good. It was a case of finding the right place to stand. Flyer started texting her friends. Maltiquor looked up intelligent trees he wanted to know more. Suddenly Maltliquor piped up and said,

"If trees are intelligent, they must know that we humans chop them down. And they may have found out that we are polluting this planet with pollutants and pesticides that are killing them. Maybe they will get really nasty when we are down there underground."

"Trust you, Maltliquor, to think of something that will scare us. We're helping them by taking back the Purple Orbs I think it's safe and we should go for it, also I want to meet Jack again," assured Flyer.

They decided to leave their tents where they were. They all put on their least liked clothes but Prancer found it hard to find anything because all of his clothes are really cool, well, that's what he thought.

Flyer picks up the box with both Purple Orbs in, then they started to walk east. Deeper into the dense wood, which was filled with different types of trees. Both Purple Orbs got brighter the further they went, suddenly both orbs went dim.

"I think we have to go back a bit," said Flyer.

Just as they turned around, Broozer's leg slipped down a hole. He then twisted and fell over into some brambles. "Ow, ow, ow, owch," he screamed as several long thorns joined to a long step clung to the back of his tee-shirt.

"Ow, Ow, get it off, Prancer, or someone, it hurts," he yelled.

Prancer took out a glove that he used for doing somersaults, then grabbed the thorny stem, pulling it off Broozer.

"Ah, thanks, Prancer, that really stuck in." Sniffled Broozer.

"That's quite a hole you've found, it's wide enough to climb in," shouted Scruffy. As Broozer pulled his leg out, only to discover his wound had opened up making his leg bleed again.

"Oh, no, my leg," Broozer shouted.

Chaffy quickly got out his medical box, then wrapped his wound.

"I think you may need some stitches in that when we get back," Chaffy said in a worried voice.

"Yer, I thought so," added Broozer.

"So who's going down first?" Maltliquor asked.

"I'll go." Volunteered Flyer.

She squeezed down the hole. It reminded her of a trip with when they went caving with a youth club.

"Pass down the box with the Purple Orbs, so I can see if it shines brighter down here," she shouted.

Both shone like purple opals with rays brighter than a star in a black evening sky.

"I have some bad news," Flyer Joked. "The Purple Orbs are shinning really brightly, so you all will have to follow me."

They all squeezed through the hole. Maltliquor and Chaffy always found anything to do with climbing, slightly difficult because of the amount of sugar they consumed. So there was a bit of huff and puffing going on. Two of them had torches but the Purple Orbs were so bright that they hardly needed them. The tunnel stared them in their eyes, there were lots of roots sticking out, which brushed against their heads. With beetles and worms in their thousands, all wriggling around. It was not really the place for The Six Macs. The ground was made of sticky red mud and it was damp and cold but it was high enough to stand up straight. There was an eeriness, together with a strange friendly feeling. Prancer got out his compass. The tunnel ran from west to east. The orb shone brighter if they walked east.

They could hear a rumbling noise which was getting louder the further east they went.

"BANG, SLAM."

"What's is that noise? It's scary," asked Maltliquor.

"Not sure," answered Prancer.

"We seem to be going downhill quite steeply." Complained Chaffy. SUDDENLY THERE WAS A LOUD BANG, THEN A CRASH just above their head. Loads of soil came crashing down on top of them, so much came down, it totally covered Broozer and Flyer. The others quickly pulled them out from the crumbling soil. The tunnel at both ends was now sealed off.

"We can't go any further. We have to turn back and I don't like that thumping noise," screamed Prancer.

"We can't go back either, we're blocked in," shrieked scruffy.

"We're goin' to be buried alive," cried Maltliquor,

"Wwwwwe are bbbburried alive," stammered Chaffy.

"We will have to dig with our hands, we still have torches and we still have both Purple Orbs. I know it's scary but we have to dig," shouted Prancer.

BANG, THUNDER, CRASH.

"Dig, dig," screamed Broozer.

After about half an hour, all the Six Macs were totally exhausted and extremely frightened.

"It's no use, we just can't dig a way out of here. I'm sure the air is getting low. I can't smell fresh air anymore," whispered Flyer.

Maltliquor had gone very quiet being too scared to talk and trying really hard not to panic. "We have to keep digging, we have to, we just can't give up," yelled scruffy. BANG, CRASH as the ground shook again.

"HELP, HELP, HELP," shouted Chaffy.

Then they all joined in. "HELP, HELP, WE'RE DOWN. HERE, HELP." Flyer was sure she heard a voice.

"Did you hear that?" asked Flyer. The others all said, "No."

"My name is Jack, Jack of the woods," Jack whispered,

"Did you hear that that time its Jack's voice?" Flyer asked them again.

The other again said, "No."

The ground started to move, they felt roots underneath them moving and twisting as if they were going to be swallowed by the ground. A hole started to appear at the end of the tunnel where they had come from earlier.

"LOOK," shouted Maltliquor who had come back into the living.

“OOOW, Maltliquor is alive.” Joked Broozer.

“Did, dig, dig,” screamed Prancer.

Soon they found themselves just below the hole that they had climbed down, all climbed out and laid onto the warm grass. It was hot and humid with loads of mosquitos buzzing around their heads.

“Wowe, that was Jack that saved us, it was I heard his voice,” Flyer cheered.

“Are you sure about that? She didn’t exactly come running to us, we could have suffocated down there.” Groaned Scruffy.

“Yer, Flyer, are you sssssure it was Jack that ssssaved us? If it was, she took her ttttime,” stammered Chaffy in a worried voice.

“You won’t get me down there again.” Sneered Maltliquor.

“But we have to go back down, we have to take back the Purple orbs,” added Flyer.

Flyer kept spitting because she got a mouthful of soil and few bits went up her nose. Scruffy’s tooth was still hurting, so he was constantly putting clove oil onto his tooth which really helped. They started walking the same way back through the woods, they could hear a loud crashing noise.

“There’s that noise, what is it?” asked Maltliquor.

Then they heard a chain saw, they all looked at each other. The crashing noise got loader, then through the woods thirty metres in front of them, they saw a yellow digger.

"That's what caused the soil to land on our heads. We were underneath where it was digging, we could have been killed," yelled Prancer.

"I think we need to go around the workmen, then find a path on the other side of them." Suggested Flyer.

So off they went keeping low in the undergrowth. Eventually, they reached the other side where they found another hole in the ground but it was slightly smaller. "No, no, no, I'm not going down another hole ever again," groaned Maltliquor.

"Nor me, not a chance," said chaffy in a scared voice.

"And I'm not too keen either," added Scruffy. Flyer put her clenched fists into the air. "Are we wee wimps or are we The Six Macs?" she shouted.

"Oh, all right." Sniffled Maltliquor, who had his head bowed, reluctantly he held his arm in the air.

Chaffy and Scruffy followed, then they all shouted, "The Six Macs."

Prancer went down first. He shouted up to the others. "It's amazing down here. I have never seen anything like it, come down and see."

Flyer went next, the other four just heard a giant loud, "WOWs."

Then Chaffy went next. He had a bit of trouble squeezing through the hole. Another 'WOW' echoed from the hole. Broozer, Scruffy and Maltliquor just wanted to get down there to see what all the fuss was about. Maltliquor also found the hole a bit on the tight side and Broozer found the hole a challenge with his bad leg but didn't complain. Eventually, they were all standing in the deep cavern about two metres high, it was more like a cave. There were roots sticking out of the soil, which were lit up like Christmas lights, some shone brighter than others. Occasionally, some roots would light up and then go out again. It looked like a giant computer system. Root after root all connected up, not only tree roots but other roots twinned together. Some roots were tiny and delicate, some were dark black while others were different shades of reds and browns. Mixed among the roots were hundreds of bright-green fluorescent glow-worms. "Were in fairyland," rejoiced Scruffy.

"Yar, hooo. Ha ha ha what did you say? Fairyland? Who believes in fairies? Scruffy does," heckles Broozer.

"Hey, Scruffy, don't move. You have something on your head," joked Flyer.

"What is it?" Scruffy said in a worried voice.

The other five all shouted, "A fairy." as they all laughed out loud.

"I didn't say I believed in fairies, I said this all looks like fairyland, there's a difference you know," stated Scruffy.

"OK, we believe you." Laughed Flyer.

Chaffy threaded carefully as he didn't want to thread on any lit roots just in case he got an electric shock.

"I suppose they're only roots, ain't they?" asked Broozer.

"Yes, but were in the sacred wood, so I think we should be more respectful and Chaffy said he got a nasty electric shock when he touched one," answered Flyer.

Scruffy suddenly said, "OWWWW, my tooth no longer hurts."

"It must have been the fairies that made it better," teased Broozer.

"I don't find you funny anymore," stressed Scruffy.

"Ooooow, OK I won't tease you again, promise." Grinned Broozer.

There was an eerie feeling but at the same time a friendly feeling floating through the air again. As they went deeper down the tunnel of lights, the Purple Orbs got brighter and so did the lit roots.

Everything was going just to plan, to their amazement in front of them, about ten metres away, it looked like the tunnel opened up. In front of them was a huge cavern brightly lit with a purple hue. There was only a short way to go when there was another giant CRASH. The tunnel in front of them totally caved in.

"Oh, no, not again," shouted Prancer. They were all a bit scared in case the roof collapsed again, so they quickly turned around and ran as fast as their legs could carry them. Forgetting about not standing on the lit-up roots, Flyer was first to get an electric shock that shot her nearer the exit, followed by all the others. The cave lit up like a firework as all of them repeatedly got electric shocks before climbed out of the hole as quick as possible. “Phew, that was lucky.” Puffed Chaffy.

“Lucky, do you call that lucky? I have never had so my electric shocks ever in my whole life.” Groaned Maltliquor.

“Well, there’s one thing that we have learned and that’s don’t stand on the roots.” Smirked Broozer.

Flyer started to cry. “What’s up?” asked Prancer.

9. Protesters

"I'm sad, aren't you? All of those beautiful lit up roots, they're all being destroyed and for what? I think we should go and take a look to see what areas they are bulldozing. The workmen may be destroying the place where the Purple Orbs live. They could destroy the Lake of Life, which will kill all trees. Also, they could be planning to cut down the old oak tree, we must stop them." Snivelled Flyer.

They had only walked about one hundred metres when they saw lots of people waving banners. They were shouting, "Save our Wood, Save our wood." They noticed that the people were wearing brightly coloured clothes. Some women had rings in their noses, some men had long hair, they were of all ages. Up in the trees, there were loads of rainbow hammocks intertwined like coloured spiders webs. Some men were in the hammocks shouting down. "Wow, loads of demonstrators. They're trying to stop the workmen, we should join in," ranted Flyer as she put her arm into the air with her fist clenched.

The other followed shouting, “The Six Macs,” all at the same time.

Prancer got his compass out. “The workmen are heading east. We have to stop them before they dig up and destroy The Lake of Life. We don’t really have any time to join in with the demonstrators.” Suggested Prancer.

Maltliquor saw something that took his mind off anything to do with woods, orbs or green women. He came out with a very strange request.

“Does anyone have any money on them?” he asked.

“Money, money, what do you need money for?” asked Scruffy.

Maltliquor pointed to a converted ambulance, written along the top it said, “Cafe Froot.” Then in smaller letters it read, “Smoothy Bar.” They all went over to it, looking inside they saw a smiley lady and a funny-looking man with a bright purple earring.

“I’ll get these. I’ll pay with my prize money. What do you want?” asked Prancer.

“One Raspberry Zinger, two Mango Tango’s, one Very Berry, one Beetroot, Carrot and Celery Juice for me and a Crunchy Whizz Shake for Maltliquor made with one whole crunchy milk and ten scoops of vanilla ice cream.”

“Oooow, these are delicious and the best I have ever tasted, great idea, Maltliquor.” Smiled Flyer.

“Yer, super brain freeze.” Giggled Maltliquor.

For ten minutes they all totally forgot about everything, their drinks were just so yummy. Scruffy only managed half of his, it started to make his tooth hurt badly.

"Well, that's done it, my tooth really hurts now." Complained Scruffy.

"You should have gone to the dentist when you had that appointment you told us about. You know the one you said that you pretended to be ill so that you didn't have to go." Slurped Broozer as he finished the last fruity lumps from the bottom of his smoothy cup.

"I just don't like going to the dentist." Complained Scruffy.

"Then stop eating your dad's cakes." Teased Chaffy. "We can bury these cups back at camp. I read a notice on that smoothy van saying 'biodegradable cups'," suggested Flyer.

It was getting late, the workmen were packing up to go home. They had put up a giant fence in front of the old oak tree on the fence it said, "BEWARE, KEEP OUT ELECTRIC FENCE." There was a smaller notice in very small writing pinned next to the sign.

"Look at this Maltliquor you're the one with the beedie-eyed glasses, what does it say?" asked Chaffy.

"It says NATURE AND MINNING OBSERVATORY granted planning permission to dig one-hundred metres deep, planning permission to build a three-storey building, planning permission to cut down all the trees in this wood."

"I can't believe it. They're going to build a nature observatory on this beautiful wood. I can't work that one out." Sighed Flyer.

There was a small track running through the wood. Scruffy noticed something shiny, then heard laughter. He sneaked through some bushed to take a look.

"Hey, you lot, take a look at this but stay low," he whispered putting his fingers up to his mouth.

They all got onto their hands and knees, then crawled over to the other side of the track through some bushes. There were five large black trucks with loads of men dressed in black, all drinking smoothies around a huge fire. Leaning against the trucks were loads of shiny clear plastic shields with about six Alsatian dogs tied to a tree.

"Who are they?" whispered Flyer.

"I think they are policemen. I reckon they're going to get rid of the demonstrators by force very soon," answered Prancer.

"Yer, it looks like it could get nasty around here, we should go." Suggested Maltliquor.

"But first we should warn the protesters," whispered Scruffy.

They all crept back into the wood to look for some protesters to tell them about what they had seen.

"Over there," shouted Chaffy MacTaffy.

They ran over to a friendly-looking man who was sitting next to a small fire with an older lady. Broozer pointed to the track.

"There are loads of policemen with trucks and Alsatian dogs over that way," he boomed without a breath.

"Yes, thank you for telling us but we already know about them. They're going to evict us from the woods tomorrow," he said.

"Well, they're going to try." Laughed the older lady.

I think we should go back to our tents to cook some food and think of a plan for tomorrow. On the way back they collected some dry wood. There was a huge old log next to a huge hole that the workmen had dug, which they thought would be really good to keep their fire burning for a long time.

"Give me a hand with this log," shouted Maltliquor.

Three of them grabbed it, then pulled it through the brown undergrowth, leaving a trail of disturbed mud and dead leaves behind them. "Yipppeee, this is goin' to be a whopper," shrieked Flyer. They lit it fairly quickly.

Suddenly Broozer shouted, "Oh, NO, an Orb, it's being burnt."

He quickly dived towards the burning fire and grabbed a small sizzling Purple Orb from a burning log. Throwing it into the air because its shell was so hot before catching it and putting it straight into his cup of water.

"It must have been living inside the log," screamed Flyer.

"Is it dead?" asked Chaffy.

"I don't know," answered Maltliquor as he prodded it with his finger.

"It's a bit shrivelled and its shell has turned black but I can see it's still moving, I think it will be fine." Assured Broozer.

"It's got to be, it can't die, trees may die if it dies, it can't die," expressed Flyer with concern.

"Let's have another look in the morning." Suggested Prancer.

Flyer volunteered to cook, her mum has taught her to cook loads of curries from recipes that have been handed down from her ancestors in India. So she has decided to make them a vegetable Bhuna made with tomatoes and spices that she has brought with her, served with rice.

While Flyer was cooking, Prancer suggest that they have a brainstorming meeting. To solve the problem to stop the workmen from destroying the wood and to return the Purple Orbs. "What's a brainstorming meeting?" asked Scruffy.

"It's when we all come up with lots of different ideas, then we choose the best one," answered Prancer.

"I've got a pen and a piece of paper," said Chaffy.

"Right then, I think we should puncher all the tyres on the digger, then get underneath it and bash up the engine," suggested Broozer.

"No, we can't do that, someone owns it. That's criminal damage, we could get put in prison," answered Prancer.

"I think we ssshould, we should be pppeaceful and lay in front of the dddigger," stammered Chaffy.

"The trouble with that is that we're smaller than the other demonstrators, so we can be picked up easier," answered Maltliquor.

"I've got it, this is the best, this is it, a guarantee, we'll be heroes." Smiled Prancer.

"Come on then, out with it?" asked Broozer,

"Wait for it, this is the one, the others went quiet waiting in anticipation. Back in the wood that is owned by Bonnie and Bruce, there are those really rare orchids. If we can get back there and dig five of them up, we could bring them back here and plant them near the old oak. The workmen would have to stop digging because they are protected. It's the same as if someone wanted to build a house in a field. If a yellow-crested newt is found on someone's land, they would be refused planning permission and not be allowed to build the house because yellow-crested newts are protected. We learned about it at school," Prancer said with pride.

"But how do we get back to the wood? We only have one day left. The wood is a good one day walk away," asked Chaffy.

"I'll do it, I've been practising for the Edinburgh marathon. I reckon I can get there and back by tomorrow morning if I leave after supper. I'm fast, trust me." Boasted Prancer.

"That sounds a fantastic idea, the best. I can just see the faces on the workmen when they see the orchids." Smiled Scruffy.

"Supper is now being served," shouted Flyer.

It looked delicious. Flyer had even put a few fresh coriander leaves on top of each curry to make it look nice. They sat around the fire. "Wow, this is the best campfire meal I have ever tasted," praised Maltliquor.

"A campfire meal is not much of a compliment. I reckon it's the best I have ever tasted, thank you, Flyer." Smiled Prancer.

"Thanks, I was a bit nervous because it's not my best, I can do a lot better using a proper cooker." Sighed Flyer.

"Book me in for your next meal when we get home." Joked Broozer.

"Prancer has a great idea," yelled Chaffy.

So Prancer told Flyer his plan. She thought it was the best plan ever. In fact, she thought it was so good, she leaned over to Prancer to give him a kiss on the cheek. Prancer went the colour of a red traffic light.

"Remind me not to come up with any good ideas." Chortled Broozer.

They all finished their curries with not one grain of rice left on their plates, Maltliquor went over the top by licking his plate clean.

"Well, I'm so pleased you enjoyed it." Beamed Flyer.

She then started to text friends to tell them about Prancer's plan. Maltliquor handed around five coke cans.

"Hey, Maltliquor, are you feeling generous for a change?" asked Scruffy.

"Yer, I thought after such nice tucker we should all have something nice to drink."

"Cheers." They all said thrusting their arms into the air, they then shouted, "To the Six Macs."

"And to Prancer," shouted Flyer.

Prancer was starting to get ready, it meant running through the night. He was feeling brave but didn't really like the thought of being right in the middle of nowhere, by himself, in the dark.

"Can I borrow your big flashlight Broozer? And can I borrow your extra-strong bright light?"

"Chaffy?" asked Prancer.

They both said, "Of course, you can."

Scruffy was playing around with a slow-worm he had found down the hole until its tail fell off.

"Ah, you see that's what happens if you play around with nature," said Flyer.

"It's supposed to drop off, it's a lizard. It thinks I'm going to eat it. It's a way of protecting its self. If I was a buzzard who was going to eat it, its tail would drop off. While the buzzard is eating its tail, it slithers off, getting away," explains Scruffy.

"Clever," Flyer replies in an impressed voice.

It was still light, Prancer reckoned that he would be able to get to the river before nightfall, making the crossing easier. So off he went with others waving goodbye.

"GO FOR IT," screamed Flyer as he disappeared into the evening light. Broozer dug a small hole, where he buried all the empty smoothy cups.

The five Macs thought they would go to the electric fence to see if they can find another hole. It was hard finding one big enough to climb down. All five looked everywhere and knew that they had only one day left to return the Purple Orbs and find the lost ones. Also, they knew if Prancer did not return in time, the workmen's digger would destroy the Lake of Life where the Purple Orbs lived. Circumstances were getting desperate, they thought that they would look on the other side of the wood away from the fence.

They came across loads of chopped down trees and had to climb over loads of stumps.

"It looks like the workmen have already been here, so I think if we find a hole we should be OK," suggested Broozer.

Flyer shouted, "I think I have found one. It's really big but there's a trunk right across it." They all ran over to it.

"We will never move that," squeaked Maltliquor who thought his voice had broken but on this occasion had reverted back to his old voice. “You’ve gone squeaky.” Laughed Broozer as Maltliquor turned pink.

“I think we should go back and think about how we can move the log.” Sniffed Chaffy who was starting to get cold.

So they started to make their way back. Scruffy pointed to a different way back which took them surprisingly past the biggest tree they have ever seen. It had a lot of banners hung all over it. ‘SAVE OUR TREES’. ‘SAVE OUR WOOD’. ‘HANDS OF THIS TREE’.

“This must be the big old oak, it’s so tall, wow, it’s Five Hundred years old.” Gushed Flyer.

“Let’s hug it to see what happens,” suggested Chaffy.

So, they all held hands with the tree in the middle. It was so wide that they had to stretch their arms out to make a full unbroken circle.

“Right, then, let’s all close our eyes.”

Then suddenly they all jumped back as if they had an electric shock without getting one.

“WOW, did you feel that?” asked Broozer.

“I really felt something, it was a sort of sadness,” yelled Chaffy. “No, I felt pain, it felt like this tree is hurting.” Gulped Flyer.

“It ccccould be because we hhhave three of the oooorbs,” stammered Chaffy.

“Or it could be because it knows tomorrow could be its last day, we have to fix this,” cried Flyer.

"I didn't think this tree stuff was so urgent but I do now. I really sensed something from that tree," sneered Maltliquor.

They were just leaving when one of the demonstrators walked be towards them.

"Hi, my name's Sam. I have been watching you. I saw you hugging that tree. I do it every night, did you feel anything? I haven't yet but I am sure I will soon," he said.

Flyer suddenly butted in with a loud wail. "No, we felt nothing trees can't communicate. They're just trees we were just playing a game." Then they made their way back.

"Why did you say that to him?" Asked Scruffy.

"We don't want to draw any attention to ourselves, just in case they interfere with us returning the Purple Orbs," answered Flyer.

When they got back they stoked the fire with dead and rotten wood that they had collected. Maltliquor is interested in star constellations, so he started pointing them to the other four.

10. Prancer's Quest

Meanwhile Prancer was having a rest, he was totally puffed out. He was thinking that he may have had pushed himself too hard. His aim was to cross the bridge in the light, now it was getting dark with the river nowhere in sight. In fact, he had a funny idea that he may have taken the wrong path. And was nervous about spending the whole night by himself in the dark. He has tried to phone the others a few times but there was no signal. And he was sure he saw some weird light in the sky like UFO's which freaked him out. He decided to carry on just to see if the river is further down the path. Very faintly he thought he could hear water as he continued sure enough the watery noise got louder.

"Yes, that took only two hours," he whispered to himself.

He must have been following the flattened down bracken that the Six Macs had flattened the day before because when the path ended in front of him was the fallen tree.

It was dusk, so he had to be careful with his footing. It was quite slippery where the water had splashed onto the rocks. He would surely drown if he fell in because it was almost dark and he would surely hit his head on a rock or something. He was just about to edge his way across when he heard laughing on the other side. Could it be the boys who they stole the orb from. *Oh, dear, what shall I do? I have to get back to the wood,* he thought.

He decided to go for it, the evening dew had settled making the fallen tree really slippery as well as very wet. Carefully he sat down on the tree, as soon as he did, he felt dew seeping through into his pants, giving him an uncomfortable feeling of a cold wet butt.

"Oh, yuk," he whispered.

He was trying to shine the torch downwards so that the boys on the other side would not see it. But things were going bad his torch was shining everywhere as he tried to slide his way across.

"Woow," he suddenly shouted as he almost lost his balance. It was a rather loud, woow.

The older boys were cooking a late supper as Prancer got further over he could hear them talking. The smell of burgers cooking on their fire wafted past his nose. Prancer was so pleased he had managed to get over without falling in the river and had not been seen by the older lads. There was one last thing to do. He had to sneak past their tents with his torch out. He could still see because it was still quite light around their tents from their roaring fire. As he started to edge his way forward, he tripped on something large lying on the ground.

"OOOOW," he shouted as he fell flat onto the cold wet grass. Frank suddenly stopped talking.

"What was that?" asked one of them as they started to walk towards Prancer.

Prancer had noticed that he had tripped over a kayak. So he was able to crawl inside it so that he was out of sight. David and Greg walked right past him, they didn't have their torches, so missed him completely. Then went back to their campfire.

"It must have been a fox or some animal," said Trevor. Prancer climbed out to the kayak really quietly.

His tummy was rumbling probably from the smell of food or maybe from Flyer's curry. He was just past the second tent when he let out the biggest loudest FART he had ever done ever. Prancer froze with fear, he heard one of the lads say,

"What was that? It came from behind your tent."

Prancer MacDancer looked up when a torch shone right into his face.

"What do we have here?" said Frank.

"I think it's Mr Farty Pants." Smirked Greg as they all laughed.

Prancer smiled, then said, "Hello." "So what are you doing sneaking around our tents?" asked Frank who spoke in a posh voice. Prancer had to make up a story really quickly. He didn't want them to find out that they were the ones that took their purple snail.

"I'm staying with my aunt and uncle. I went camping with my friends and I forgot my sleeping bag. So I was going back to get it," Prancer explained.

"What are your aunt's and uncle's names? We might know them." David asked.

Prancer had forgotten Chaffy's uncle's name. "My aunt is called Bonnie," answered Prancer.

"And your uncle's name?"

"I've only met him twice, I can't remember." Lied Prancer.

"So what's your name?" asked Greg.

He couldn't give him the secret Six Macs name, so he told them his real name.

"My name is Glenn," Prancer said.

"Well, Glenn, I think you're lying. I'm staying with my Poppa and Nanna. Their next-door neighbours are called Bonnie and Bruce. They told my Poppa and Nanna that their nephew was coming to stay but his name wasn't Glenn." Snarled Greg.

"Why are you lying to us eeeer?" asked Trevor.

Prancer froze, he didn't really know what to say, then he came totally clean.

"All right, all right, I will tell you the truth but I'm not sure that you will believe me. I will start at the beginning, so he told them everything." After about ten minutes one of the lads interrupted.

"So you're the ones who stole our snail but really I don't blame you, we didn't leave any food for it. We found it stuck to a bulldozer outside my Nanna and Poppa's house, which is about three miles from here. It had stopped at some traffic lights in front of my Poppa's drive, it was so unusual we decided to keep it. We put it in the hole so that we could look it up in a book to see what type of snail it was," explained David. The lads were friendly to Prancer's relief.

"My name is David, that's Frank, that's Trevor and lastly, that's Greg. We're all from Petersfield, apart from Greg, here's a Scott. I'm not really sure whether I believe all of your stories but can we help in any way?" asked David.

"No, I'm a really good runner, so I will catch up with you on my return. Goodbye, I must go now." Insisted Prancer.

With a flip of a heel, he shot off into the blackness of the night, a little scared because there was no moon. Eerie shadows appeared the disappeared as his torch shone onto bushes and trees. He could hear in the distance noises from a barking fox. Now and then he would disturb a bird with would make a sudden flutter noise in the trees, which made him JUMP OUT OF HIS SHOES. He was sure an owl was following him which gave out the occasional squawk.

11. Recued Orbs

Back at The Six Mac's camp, the other five were getting tied. Chaffy had just changed Broozer's bandage.

"Your legs getting better. I think you should take the bandage off tomorrow to let your wound breathe," suggested Chaffy.

Flyer was texting, she was also trying to phone Prancer but there was no signal. Maltliquor was playing games on this phone while drinking a can of coke and eating a jam doughnut which had gone a bit stale. Scruffy was hanging upside down just above Maltliquor trying to tickle his nose with a piece of long grass.

"Go way away, Scruffy, go and annoy someone else." Sniffled Maltliquor.

Broozer put some leaves into the Tupperware container to feed both Purple Orb. Their shells were shining really brightly. The burnt one was moving but its shell was very dim.

"I'll keep them with me tonight if that's OK?" asked Broozer.

"Yes, that's fine," answered Flyer.

"Wouldn't it be weird if trees are intelligent? Just think of all that money that is being spent by the governments from all over our world, who are sending rockets into space to look for intelligent species on other worlds. When all along there here right underneath their noses," Maltliquer suggested.

"Yer, I think Flyer is right, just because trees don't communicate like us, it doesn't mean that they aren't intelligent. In fact, they are the perfect pacifist they kill nothing to survive and give life to others by purifying our air. What do you think of that Flyer?" asked Broozer.

"I really think you have something I think we should do some serious research when we get back home," answered Flyer.

"Yes, got it, it's all coming together. First, it starts with a bright moon, which gives energy to the Purple Orbs. Then the Purple Orbs transfer their energy into the great Lakes of Life. The trees with their huge root, then feed from the Lake of Life, which gives them energy to grow, who in-turn feed our planet with purified air that keeps everything alive, perfect!" exclaimed Maltliquor with a smile.

"Then along came man, who has messed everything up," added Broozer.

"Broozer, you're not normally philosophical, maybe all of this green woman stuff is getting to you." Interrupted Flyer.

"Yer, it could be. I can't see why we always have to dig and destroy. Wouldn't it be nice if we all lived in tents?" added Broozer.

"It would be cold in the winter." Shivered Maltliquor.

"Yer, I suppose so," said Broozer, who hadn't really thought out his answer property because he was tired.

"I think we should go to bed so that we can get up really early," suggested Flyer, who had now finished texting her friends.

So off they went after brushing their teeth, Scruffy thought he would leave brushing his teeth until the next morning.

Prancer stopped for a while because he could see lights shining in the distance. Also, more disturbing he could hear gunshots like cracks of thunder in a distant sky. The shots he could hear he thought must be from poachers shooting rabbits or deer. He thought that there was a strong chance that they could shoot him by mistake, so he froze perfectly still. As the gunshots became louder, Prancer knew that they were getting nearer to him. He was really scared, so he cowered on the floor next to a fallen tree stump. He could hear something running towards him, something big and it was making a barking squeaking noise. Suddenly, a huge deer jumps over the stump, he was cowering against. With even louder gunshots almost deafening. "BANG, Bang, BANG." There seemed to be five or six men, all shouting. There was so much noise for a few minutes but it felt like an hour.

Then they were gone as fast as they had arrived with the sound of gunshots disappearing into the night. Prancer was shaking with fear. “Phew, that was a close one,” whispered Prancer as he jumped up to continue running. Not feeling scared any more, knowing that he was not alone in the woods. He knew he had nearly reached his destination when he came across a wet soggy patch in the field near where the pond was.

“Great, ten more minutes to go, then I’m going to have a long rest.” Dreamed Prancer. When he arrived he thought that he would have a sleep as he rolled out his sleeping bag, he tucked himself under a bush, then fell fast asleep.

Broozer woke up abruptly. He could hear noises coming from Flyers tent, she was screaming,

“Please, leave me alone, please, leave me alone.”

Broozer woke up the others. “Wake up, Chaffy, wake up, Maltliquor,” he shouted.

“What’s all the noise?” Groaned sleepy Scruffy.

“It’s Flyer. She is having a bad dream,” whispered Broozer while putting his fingers up to his mouth.

Surprisingly, they saw Flyer climb out of her tent. She then started to walk into the woods with only her pyjamas on.

“Quickly get dressed, we should follow her,” shrieked Chaffy.

"I'll stay here, I'll look after the camp," shuddered Maltliquor.

"NO, you're coming with us. Don't be such a wimp." sneered Broozer.

Flyer was walking very slowly, so it took quite a long time getting to the other side of the wood.

They saw her climb down a hole, the other stayed above ground peering into the hole, where they could hear talking. Flyer found herself in another dream, she was with Jack again. "Do you remember me? I'm Jack, Jack of the wood. I am your friend. I've come to give you a message. You must get my Purple Orbs back into my Lake of Life by midnight tonight. It's a night of a full moon, you must help my Purple Orbs to return. Or else all my trees in this wood and other woods will start to die and I will start to fade. Also, you must protect the wise old oak tree. He is over five hundred years old. He is a very wise tree who has many more years to live, he is my old friend. We have experienced many moons together, you must help me or I will fade," whispered Jack.

All of a sudden Flyer woke up, Jack disappeared as quickly as she had arrived.

She found herself underground again, in fright she gave an almighty scream: "SCREEEEEEEEEAM."

"It's all right, Flyer, we're here. Flyer, stretch your arms up, so we can pull you up," shouted Scruffy.

Flyer stretched her arms out, then Scruffy pulled her out, she was shaking from fright and cold.

"I saw Jack again. She said we have until midnight to get the orbs back into the Lake of Life. Also, we have to save the wise old oak tree." Insisted Flyer in a wobbly voice.

It was only four-thirty in the morning but it was starting to get light. The five Macs knew they had a long challenging day ahead of them, so decided not to go back to bed.

"I wish we hadn't found that Purple Orb now Jack scares me but what scares me even more is that if we don't get all the Purple Orbs back tonight, all our beautiful trees will die. And it's all down to us to fix it," Flyer said in a worried voice.

"Oh, come on, this is a real adventure. How many others have seen the Green woman?" asked Maltliquor.

"Yer, but you haven't had one of their dddreams or ended up down a hole with a ssscary wooden gggreen woman looking at you, have you?" added Chaffy.

"In fact if you had, you would be scared out of your pants right now." Sniggered Broozer.

"In fact, I don't think you would even be here." Joked Scruffy.

"Yer, you would probably be halfway home in your pyjamas." Teased Broozer.

"That's a bit harsh." Objected Maltliquor.

"Are you all right, Flyer?" asked Broozer.

“Yes, I’m fine now, thank you,” answered Flyer.

“Let’s go back to our tents, it’s cold. We could light a fire,” suggested Scruffy, who did like lighting fires.

After getting back they checked the Purple Orbs to see if it needed more water and vegetation to eat and to see if the burnt one was still alive. Broozer prodded it with his finger. It was totally dead. “Oh, no, it’s died,” cried Flyer.

“Look, what is that in the corner? It looks like a glowing yellow pearl. It’s so bright for such a small thing,” said Chaffy.

“It an egg, Jack said the dead one orb would lay an egg before it died. It’s a way of controlling the Purple Orbs population, it’s how the Lake of Life has stayed stable for millions of years.” Smiled Flyer.

“Wow, we really have to look after them. We have to find the rest, maybe we can get Jack to help,” suggested Broozer.

“It’s such a bright yellow glow. I think it has connections to Jacks spirit.” Smiled Flyer.

“The other two Purple Orbs lights were very dull, I think they’re dying.” Gasped Chaffy.

“Oh, no, they can’t die. Please, don’t die, little snails,” whispered Flyer in a worried voice, as she stroked their shells.

“It’s not long now we’ll get you back on time, we will, won’t we, gang?” asked Chaffy as he held his arm in the air with his fist clenched, the other did the same and they shouted, "The Six Macs."

Scruffy noticed a slight purple glow next to Flyers tent.

"Hey, look, what are these? There are four Purple Orbs, where have they come from?" asked Scruffy.

"They were probably in the log that we burnt. They must have slithered out before we put it onto last night's fire," answered Broozer.

"So what are they doing next to flyer's tent?" Queried Maltliquor.

"Look, they're all on top of where I buried the smoothy cups. Scruffy's half drank smoothly is buried there as well, maybe they like Raspberries," answered Flyer.

"That was really lucky we found Cafe Froot or we may never have found the other Purple Orbs." Smiled Scruffy.

"Yer, and it's a good job. Your tooth was aching, talking about your tooth have the fairies stopped it aching again?" asked Broozer.

"Stop teasing him, or I may not bandage your leg," laughed Chaffy.

12. The Orchid

Prancer woke up with a fright. He could feel something crawling around his feet at the bottom of his sleeping bag. He couldn't get out quick enough but his zip was caught on a piece of nylon and it was stuck.

"Eeeeeeek," he shouted as he wriggled around.

The zip suddenly broke free, so he was able to climb out, quickly tipping his sleeping bag upside down. A little scared mouse plopped on to some green moss, then scurried off into the undergrowth. Prance looked down at his socks. There was a large, chewed hole in one of his socks, where the little mouse must had been nibbling his toes. Prancer scratched his head, then suddenly jumped up.

"OH, NO, it's light, it's morning, WHAT, What's the time? Oh, no I'm supposed to be running back. Oh no, I'm late," he stressed.

Prancer got his spade from out of his rucksack which was wrapped in a polythene bag. As he made his way over towards the orchids, he could hear Chaffy's aunt and uncle voices. Prancer dived into some bushes, unfortunately for him he dived into some holly bushes which were camouflaging the orchids. Deep inside his head he wanted to shout 'AAAAAAAAAH' but he had to keep quiet. There was a particularly sharp holy leaf sticking right into his butt, so he tried to manoeuvre himself by raising his butt off the ground. But it just wasn't working. *Ow, Ow, Ow,* he was thinking.

Bruce and Bonnie were walking their dog a cock-a-poo called Daisy, it was a sweet dog. Prancer really liked it, it was a very friendly dog. Daisy ran straight over to Prancer, then started barking after dropping a pork chop it had found under a bush.

"Go away, Daisy, please, go away," he whispered, as it licks Prancer's nose leaving a stale pork chop smell behind. Prancer hated being licked by dogs, especially on the face.

"Please, go away, please," as he pats her head.

The holly leaf was stuck in the worst place ever, he just wanted them to go away, so he could move.

"Daisy," shouted Bruce.

"What have you found?" asked Bonnie as she started to walk towards Prancer.

"No, no, no, go away, Daisy," whispered Prancer in a worried voice.

Suddenly Daisy saw a squirrel. With a bark she was gone, Bruce shouts to Bonnie,

"Come on, Bonnie, it was probably another squirrel. We should get back home, we have a lot to do and we don't want to spook the campers."

Phew, that was a close one, now where are those orchids? thought Prancer. He rolled over carefully so that he could remove the holly leaf from his butt. "Ow, that hurt," he mumbled.

"Ah, there they are."

They all looked really beautiful but then he noticed another pork chop which was sitting right in the middle of them which spoilt the beauty. He dug each one out carefully, individually wrapping them, then put the beautiful delicate flowers into his bag. A sausage roll breakfast washed down with a carton of orange juice, was perfect for the energy he needed to get back. He filled in the holes, then put some twigs on top to disguise the disturbed foliage.

He then jumped up, then headed off. He had to move fast. He cleared the first five fences by leaping straight over them, by placing one hand on top of each. Clearing them by at least a quarter of a metre, his shoe caught a length of barbed wire at fence six, throwing him over into a freshly dumped cow-pat. He also landed badly twisting his bad ankle. He wasn't sure whether to cry out in pain or cry out pooooooooooooooooooo. It came out with a sort of

"POOOOOOOOO…AAAAHHHHHHH."

There was no water around anywhere and he couldn't walk, not for a toffee. Prancer sat there for about ten minutes, thinking of different options with nasty orange flies buzzing around his arms and tee shirt, while seated he checked the orchids they were fine. After his rest he managed to stand up, to his delight his ankle wasn't broken. He could just walk but with a hobble but it was painful.

It was probably only about two miles away from the river where he was hoping that David and his mates would still be camping. He found a thick stick, so he used it to walk with. All he could think of is, will he get back on time? After a long hobble, eventually, he could hear running water but had to have a rest. As he started to sit down, he suddenly jumped up again that holly leaf had given him a really sore butt. He started to think and started to feel very sorry for himself.

"I'm on holiday, I've got a sore butt, a bad ankle. I'm covered in poo and I probably won't be able to run the Edinburgh marathon this year, is this all worth it."

He was not very happy which is very unusual for Prancer, he tried to phone each one of The Six Mac's but there was no signal. Just at that point, he heard Frank shout,

"That's a big one reel in it."

Prancer gave out an almighty shout, "Frank, HEEEEELPPPP!" He waited for a couple of seconds.

"Glenn, where are you?" shouted Frank.

"I'm here, I'm here, I'm behind these rocks, I've hurt my ankle," screamed Prancer.

"WOW, Glenn, you look poooped, grab my arm. I'll help you down to the river, so you can wash that poo off," suggested Frank.

Prancer told them about why he must get the orchids back.

"I have to plant them before the workmen start using their diggers, their diggers will destroy the Lake of Life, which is home to the Purple Orbs. They have protected trees for centuries.

"We just can't let it happen, we just have to get back," explained Prancer. Prancer was drying off when David said,

"We'll help with two of us, one each side of you we'll almost fly there."

"Great, fantastic, it should only take a couple of hours." Thanked Prancer.

David and Trevor grabbed Prancer's arms, then off they went. Prancer was hardly touching the ground, they were really moving fast, just a quarter of an hour had passed when Prancer suddenly shouted, "WHERE'S MY BAG?"

He had left next to where he was washing. Greg suggested that they continued while he ran back to retrieve Prancer's bag.

“At the speed we’re going, we should be there under two hours if nothing else goes wrong,” shrieked Prancer who had just banged his foot on a stone with an ‘Ow’.

They were all getting a bit worried, Greg had not caught up with them and a whole hour had passed. “Where do you think Greg is? He should have been with us by now,” asks Prancer.

“He’ll be here soon. He helps out with the scouts, he’s excellent at finding his way around,” explained Trevor.

They were walking along a wooded path, then just in front of them was Greg sitting high up in a tree.

“Hi, I’m pretending to be a fridge, what kept you?” He joked.

“What do you mean pretending to be a fridge?” asked Prancer.

“We found a fridge full of food hanging up in a tree back at Chaffy’s aunt and uncles wood, was it anything to do with you?” asked Greg.

“Maltliquor,” shouted Prancer.

“Maltliquor, what do you mean by Maltliquor?” quizzed David.

“Oh, nothing. A friend of mine was supposed to have buried the fridge. It sounds like he didn’t bury it but instead hung in a tree. I wondered how he dug a huge hole so quickly, had all the food fallen out?” asked Prancer.

"No, but when we got it down, we helped ourselves to what was left. It was very good, thank you. Especially those sausages hidden behind the pork chops," answered Frank.

"Oh, well, they're gone now. GOT YOU, Maltliquor," Prancer whispered under his breath. His foot was starting to hurt again but there was one good thing the prickliness on his butt had gone.

"I think we should get going," suggested Prancer.

13. The Lake of Life

Flyer was checking all the Purple Orbs. They were getting very dull, she started to talk to them.

"Don't worry, we promise we will get you all back today." Smiled Flyer.

The other had finished breakfast. It wasn't a very nice day, it was starting to drizzle, so they put on their waterproofs. Broozer started to dampen down the fire but gave up when it started to rain. "I think we should head for those fields over there, the route will take us around the woods.

"We don't want to bump into any policemen or anyone who will stop us returning the Orbs.

"We can then look for that hole over on the other side," suggested Flyer MacHigher. They had to climb over quite a few barbed wire fences where they kept getting their scarves caught. Chaffy ripped a hole in his which made him unhappy for a few minutes. Flyer's scarf was new, so she wrapped hers five times around her neck which made her very hot. They sneaked into the undergrowth where they could hear people shouting. In fact, it was very noisy, there were chain saws varooming, diggers banging, demonstrators shouting, "SAVE OUR WOOD" and even louder banging noises of police banging their shields.

"Wow, how are we going to climb anywhere underground, it's scary," whimpered Maltquior.

"We just have to go for it. Look, there's that hole we found yesterday." Pointed Flyer.

"Look, here is another hole, it's slightly bigger," blurted Chaffy.

It was still raining, everything was soaking wet. There was an eerie white mist floating past trees and ferns. The hole didn't look inviting whatsoever, it had a wet shinning shimmer to it.

"That's a wee hole. I'll never get down that and Prancer has our spade." Fretted Chaffy.

"Me too. I'll never get down that wee hole," added Maltliquor as he hissed open his last can of coke.

"Hey, Presto," shouted Broozer as he pulled out his Frisbee.

"That's no good." Laughed scruffy.

"I'm going to give it a go." Snapped Broozer.

He started scooping the wet soil until it was big enough for two of them to get down at once.

"There you go, there's no excuse now. We can all go down whose first?" he asked. Chaffy and Maltliquor looked at each other. They didn't want to go down. Flyer was first to jump down.

"Wow, it's fantastic down here, all the roots are lit up in different colours and it's like being in a cave, come down, come down now."

Broozer was next down followed by Scruffy, Chaffy reluctantly climbed down, then lastly Maltliquor. They all looked at each other, then laughed. They were covered in mud from head to toe. Because Maltliquor was last down he was the muddiest he even had mud in his ears and his bright orange glasses were a dirty brown colour.

"Wow, it's bright down here and look at the Tupperware box, it looks like it's on fire with a bright purple light." Gasped Scruffy.

"WOWee, look at those tree roots. They're flashing on and off in sequence. They look so alive, the lights seem brighter than in the last tunnel. We must be closer to The Lake of Life here. Wow, look over, what's that wrapped around the tree roots? It's fantastic, it's so beautiful," expressed Flyer with glee.

"Yes, it's beautiful. It looks like different coloured algae. I wish Prancer was here to see it," added Chaffy.

They all started to take pictures with their phones.

"If we get this on the internet, I'll have ten million views," shrieked Maltliquor.

They started walking further down the hole, which went around a bend without touching the lights. They were heading towards a horrible loud noise from a digger. Every so often, chunks of soil fell on top of them.

"This is so dangerous. Any minute we could end up with loads of soil on top of us. We could be killed, it's so scary." Moaned Maltliquor. All the Purple Orbs were getting even brighter, so were the roots which were starting to make a strange very quiet humming noise. "Listen, what making that noise?" asked Scruffy MacTuffy.

"I'm not sure, it's coming from all around us," answered Chaffy.

Suddenly there was a loud bang, the whole tunnel shook, mud covered them all.

"Come on, we must hurry the workmen are getting closer," Flyer bellowed, then asked, "Did you hear me?"

The others all shouted, "Yes."

Flyer suddenly stopped there in front of her were loads of thick black roots going deep down into the earth. It was a lot wider than the tunnel they had been walking along. Also, it wasn't lit, it was as black as black. The roots were twisted and twinned around each other, some were as thick as small trees, which were about fifty centimetres across. They looked wet and slippery.

As they shone their torches down further into the dark void, all five could see lots of smaller roots totally lining its walls, which were peppered with large rocks that jutted out, making it a treacherous climb down.

"I'm not going down there," cried Maltliquor.

"Look! The Orbs are getting even brighter. We must go down there." Pleaded Flyer.

"We can't give up now, we have to go down, so I'm with Flyer." Agreed Broozer.

"OK, we're in," said Chaffy.

Maltliquor looked at Chaffy with a scoured face. They all looked down the hole. It didn't look very inviting. Maltliquor wanted some reassurance, so he stopped, then shone his torch on his stretched arm with a clenched fist. Broozer smiled, then they all raised their arm then shouted, "The Six Macs." Even though there were only five of them.

Prancer had just arrived back at camp. He wondered where the others were. He thought that it would be best if he waited for them. David had a camping gas stove, so he lit it so that he could boil a kettle to make some tea. They were all fairly tired after rushing without a break for the last two hours. Bruce suggested that they should all go for a look around. Prancer decided to have another wee brew.

Flyer was feeling brave. She sort of wished that Jack was there to help but then thought that maybe she is watching. Flyer decided to go first, the black roots were really slippery. The others followed at a distance. They could hear dripping water everywhere, some roots were so tightly twisted together that they found it hard to continue. With each step they went deeper, then it seemed to change direction to STRAIGHT DOWN.

"I hope we're not doing this for nothing. I hope we're not just really bonker coming down here because if something goes wrong, no one knows we're here," complained Maltliquor. Just in that second Flyer slipped disappearing out of sight as she fell, she let go of the box with the Purple Orbs in, which landed just in front of Chaffy. Before he could grab hold of it, it slid off the root, then it also disappeared further down into the tunnel.

"Flyer, are you all right?" shouted Scruffy.

Flyer had banged her head knocking herself out while unconscious Jack of the wood visited her.

"Get up, you must get up. You have left three Purple orbs in the wood. You must get them, you must bring them back here, fallen from a log, just fallen, bring them back," she whispered in Flyers ear.

Flyer rubbed her head, then opened her eyes. The Purple Orbs was next to her, still in the plastic box. She shone her torch in front of her to see the most amazing sight. For a second she thought that she was still unconscious. She found herself standing on the edge of an enormous underground lake which shone bright purple. There were thousands of snail-like Purple Orbs shining beneath a crystal clear mass of water. From everywhere there were thick black roots sinking into the deep pure water. Around the edge there were millions of different coloured algae. It was the most beautiful sight she had ever seen.

Flyer shouted to the other, "Come down here, take a look at this, it's amazing, it's beautiful, I could meditate down here for hours." The others caught up with Flyer with amazement they couldn't believe their eyes, immediately they started taking loads and loads of pictures. They opened the Tupperware box, then submersed it into the clear water, then tipped out all the Purple Orbs including a very tiny one that had just hatched. They all floated for a few seconds, then sank slowly right to the bottom, joining hundreds of other Purple Orbs right down into the depths of a purple beautifulness. There was an energy that none of them could describe. It was all around them. Also, there was an undertone hum that made them feel relaxed as if they wanted to float through the air in a translucent bubble skimming across the purple lake.

"Woow, we have to get out of here. I have this strange sleepy warm wanting to stay feeling, what about you?" asked Broozer.

"Me too." Yawed Maltliquor.

"I'm really tired, could we just stay for a short rest? I'll set my alarm just in case we fall asleep. Ooow, I'm sooo tired," whispered Chaffy.

"I suppose we could just for a while, I'm very sleepy." Insisted Scruffy.

"No, we can't go to sleep when I hit my head. I think I knocked myself out. I think when I was unconscious, Jack visited me. She said we have left behind three Purple Orbs, and something about fallen from a log. What do you think she meant?" asked Flyer.

“Maybe all of them were together in that large log, then when we dragged it back to camp, three Purple orbs fell out,” suggested Broozer.

“Oh, I’m so tired, I just want to sleep.” Pleaded Chaffy.

“Me too,” added Maltquior.

“Well, I think me, Broozer and Scruffy should go back to look for the other three Orbs while you two have a sleep. We’ll leave our bags with you so that we can move quicker. What do you think Broozer and Scruffy?” asked Flyer.

“Good plan,” said Scruffy.

Broozer was on his way out already. It was hard going climbing up and very slippery. Broozer bashed his head twice on the sticking-out rocks, adding to the pain in his leg. Flyer’s skateboarding skills made it easier for her to climb up. Once out they noticed that all the shouting in the wood had stopped, the only noises they could hear were the sounds of chainsaws and diggers which was a bit worrying. They headed straight over to where they had found the log. “I am sure it was somewhere around here, what do you think?” asked Scruffy.

There were loads of bulldozer tyre tracks.

“If they are around here, I hope those bulldozers have not run over any of them over.” Gasped Flyer.

"Look over, there's the scrape mark we left in the soil from dragging the log back to camp. We should look over there near those rotten logs," suggested Scruffy.

Broozer started to lift a load of old dirty branches and rotten bits of wood putting them onto a new pile that he had started while Scruffy and Flyer searched the bracken but there was no sign of them.

"Maybe we should be looking further over that way," suggested Flyer.

"This is impossible. How are we going to find tiny snails in such a large wood? It's just impossible." Fretted Broozer.

They looked and looked for quite a while but they found nothing.

"We should get back to the other two," Flyer said in a disappointed voice. Just at that moment, they all heard a tapping noise.

"What's that noise?" asked Flyer.

They peered over some stacked logs and there, to their horror, was a blackbird. With one of the Purple Orbs in its beak, it was bashing its shell on a stone trying to break it, so it could eat the snail.

Broozer shouted, "BOOOOO."

The blackbird flew off, leaving the very dull Purple Orb behind. Stuck tight on a stone were the other two Purple Orbs.

"Got them," screamed Flyer with joy.

They put all three Orbs into Flyer's plastic box, then looked at the one that nearly got eaten. It looked fine apart from a couple of broken bits of shell around the edge of its shell and it was still alive. It had been raining quite hard, so they were all wet and weren't looking forward to climbing down a muddy hole. As they were climbing down towards Chaffy and Maltliquor, they heard Maltliquor shouting in a panic-stricken voice. They rushed their descent, jumping down a few final roots straight into water that covered their boots, where they found two drenched friends.

Maltliquor said, "Jack of the wood entered my dream. I remember everything, it was so real and frightening. She said to me, 'You must stop our wood being destroyed, help us, help us. Now WAKE up, you must wake up, it's raining, WAKE UP. The next thing I knew I was shouting Chaffy, Chaffy wake up and I was spluttering, I thought I was drowning.' The lake of life had got bigger."

"Yuk, my feet are soaked," screeched Flyer.

"Yer, I'm really wet." Groaned Chaffy.

"I'm so pleased I saw Jack. She told me to wake up and that it's raining. Now I know what she meant, we were both asleep laying down, we could have drowned. I'm so pleased I saw jack, she saved us." Sniffled Maltliquor, who still had some water up his nose.

"Yes, you told us," mentioned Broozer.

"But what did she mean?" asks Flyer,

"I know if it's raining up there, all the water is coming down here. That's why we're wet, it's going to flood again, we have to get out," shouted Scruffy.

"But first we have to put the Purple Orbs into the lake." Flyer insisted.

Flyer waded past Chaffy, then Flyer carefully emptied the three Purple Orbs into the crystal water, all three sank slowly into an energy-filled deep purple lake.

"My torch isn't working, it's got wet," complained Chaffy.

"Don't worry, mine is still working. I'll go up the front," insisted Flyer.

They managed to get back up into the smaller tunnel quite quickly which had turned into a stream about thirty centimetres deep. Flyer looked back. "Look, look," she screeched.

"That's scary," shouted Maltliquor.

They could see loads of slowly moving black tree roots knotting and twisting together, totally sealing up the hole they had just climbed out of. The alley down to the lake was no more. They could hear loud crashing noises above, so they scurried like frightened badger's towards the hole that they had come down. As they started to climb out all the root lights went out. Flyer was first out, followed by the rest of them. They ran as fast as possible back to their camp the same way that they had come, where Prancer was waiting for them.

14. Walking Home

Flyer greeted Prancer, then shouted with her fist in the air.

"Yay, hay, hay, we did it. We found all the Purple Orbs, we put them all back. You missed something so beautiful."

She then continued to tell Prancer her whole story which took about ten minutes. Then she noticed that Prancer was limping. "What's wrong with your foot?" asked flyer MacHigher.

"I fell badly while jumping over a gate, I don't think I will be running in the Edinburgh marathon this year." Sighed Prancer as he hobbled towards his tent. Just at that moment Trevor and Frank appeared.

"Hi, Glenn," sneezed Trevor who was suffering badly from hay fever.

The others looked frightened because they recognised the lads from Chaffy's uncle's wood.

"Hey, be cool guys, these are my friends they almost carried me here, that is David, that's Trevor and that's Frank and Greg and they know why we're here." Smiled

Prancer. The others decided to tell them their gang names because they didn't like using their real names while on holiday. Greg thought their Mac names were cool, Trevor and Frank sniggered. "Wow, that's a cool tartan tent. Have I never seen one like that before? Where did you buy it?" asked Greg.

"I stuck loads of waterproof tartan material over it," answered Flyer proudly.

"You did a really good job," Greg added.

"Thank you." Blushed Flyer.

"We don't have long, did you get the orchids Prancer?" Smiled Flyer.

"Yes, here they are," as he took them out of his bag.

They were all in one piece, not one flower was missing. David peered over Prancer's shoulder.

"Cor, they're really beautiful and so delicate, I have never seen an orchid before."

"We need a plan." Boomed Broozer, who wanted to be heard.

"I don't think we should construct a plan until we know where they are digging," suggested Frank.

"OK, let's go and take a look," added Flyer.

Prancer wanted to contribute his thoughts but decided to stay and rest his foot. Noises of chainsaws got louder as they made their way through the woods.

"There must be at least ten men using chainsaws and their moving fast," whispered Flyer.

They sneaked on their hands and knees so no one would see them.

"Look, they only have eight metres to go until they reach the old oak tree were never going to stop them," shouted Maltliquor.

"SHHHHHHHHHush," they all whispered.

"Look at that. They're bringing in some massive diggers," added Broozer.

"Now we can make a plan up." Insisted Frank.

As Flyer turned around, her head banged into a leg. It was a leg that she didn't recognise and it smelt funny, it had an earthy stinky smell. She immediately looked up and so did the others. There standing tall was a large man, they were all puzzled because they had not heard him approaching them.

"So what do we have then?" He snarled.

Before he could say anything else they all jumped up and ran as fast as their legs could take them. Maltliquor was the most frightened one, he was also the slowest and he nearly got caught.

They all arrived back at camp, Chaffy and Maltliquor were puffed out.

"That was fun," shouted David.

Trevor wasn't so sure, nor were the other five Macs. Even though Prancer had not been with them, he said, "I've been thinking very hard. I think I have a really good plan but first we have to phone the Rare Orchid Society."

"I'll phone," suggested Flyer as she took out her phone.

"Oh, no, it's soaking wet, it's ruined. I left it in my bag down by the Lake of Life, did you leave yours in your bag Scruffy?" asked Flyer.

"Yes, I did, so did Broozer," answered Scruffy.

The other four checked their phones all of them were wet. "Oh, no, all of our pictures are gone, nobody will believe us now," ranted Maltliquor.

Prancer announced his plan, "We have to plant the orchids in three different places. It has to look like this wood is the perfect habitat for this type of orchid to survive. I found this information on my phone while you were away. I think we have until tomorrow night."

Flyer interrupted, "No, we don't have that long. We saw them bringing some gigantic diggers in. They're going to trash the wood tomorrow. They'll destroy the Lake of Life, killing the purple Orbs, then everything will die including the old oak tree and Jack will fade forever." She stressed.

"I think we should plant them some tonight and the rest first thing tomorrow morning. After we have planted them we can ring The Rare Orchid Society," suggested Trevor.

"No, I will phone them now, their office is in Liverpool, so hopefully they will turn up tomorrow morning," interrupted Prancer.

"What about the electric fence?" enquired Frank.

"I think if we go around it through the fields, we can get on the other side without going anywhere near the fence," suggested Broozer.

They decided to wait until dusk, so they cooked up some beans, in fact that's all they had left.

David cooked four trout that his friends had caught that morning before Prancer turned up, which they shared with the Six Macs but fish and beans didn't really taste that good.

Maltliquor opened a can of coke. "Hey, Maltliquor, I thought you said that you had drunk your last can, so where did you get that one from?" asked Chaffy.

"I stocked up at that Cafe Froot smoothy bar." He smiled.

"Typical, you spend all your money on coke-a-cola, you'll end up fat as a house." Joked Prancer.

"Go on, give us one. You can get more tomorrow?" asked Broozer. Maltliquor threw one over to Broozer MacDoozer.

Dusk came around really quickly. Prancer's foot was a lot better, thanks to Chaffy, who had wrapped his foot tight with a bandage. Prancer has decided to go along with them. They have all agreed to plant the first one very near to the fence behind the old oak tree. After climbing over all the barb-wired fences, without ripping any of their scarfs, they all arrived at the edge of the wood where there was loads of wet bracken. After a short walk, they found themselves inside the fence which was being controlled by security guards with dogs. The security guards were sitting down, one of them looked as if he was asleep. It was probably because all the demonstrators had been cleared away. As they got closer, one of the dogs started to bark, instantly a security guard shone a really bright torch towards them.

"DUCK," whispered Flyer.

"Where?" whispered Prancer.

"Only joking." She smiled.

Prancer gave Flyer a light slap on his back. They all laid low, Prancer sneaked forward on his hand and knees with his spade. He then dug a small hole in the soil, before carefully planting his first orchid.

"He's brave," said Trevor.

"He's a hero, he's one of The Six Mac's," answered Flyer with pride. Prancer sneaked back.

"Only four more to go," he bragged.

They all then crawled back towards the dark wood, carefully avoiding lots of prickly brambles.

As they passed the old oak tree, Flyer said, " you are my favourite tree ever. I can feel your friendly spirit, I love you, tree. Don't worry we will save you, and this beautiful wood."

"We have to plant two orchids right above where the lake of life is, do you know where it is?" queried Prancer.

"Yes, sort of, if we can find the hole that we went down, we can work out roughly where it is."

“I think it’s somewhere over there,” answered Flyer, as she pointed.

They spent about an hour looking for the hole but seemed to be going around in circles. It had got a lot darker, and was almost pitched black with no moon. None of them couldn’t shine a torch, just in case they were spotted by a guard.

“This is mad, we just can’t find it, we will have to come back when it’s lighter,” suggested Maltliquor.

“We can’t go back. We might get caught. Anyway, we’re here now, I think we should sit it out. It will be starting to get light in about four hours,” whispered Frank.

“OK but I think we should still continue looking for the hole, we should split up into pairs. Whoever finds the hole should stay by it, whoever doesn’t find it meets back here in four hours,” Prancer said in a confident low voice.

Only ten minutes had passed when Chaffy and Broozer found the hole.

“WOW, that was quick. I should have been more fffforcefull in sssuggesting the hole was this way. I had a sssstrange idea it was this way,” stammered Chaffy, who was starting to feel tired.

“We can go to sleep now for a few hours,” added Broozer.

“No way am I going asleep near tttthat hole. I’m not letting Jack get into my dreams, she’s spooky. I’m ssstaying awake all night,” stressed Chaffy.

The others were in different parts of the wood, all looking in the wrong places. Dusk came around very slowly, Chaffy suddenly woke up, so did Broozer. Both had succumbed to tiredness and were wet from morning dew.

“What’s that noise?” Coughed Broozer who was clearing his throat.

He was sure a spider or something creepy crawly had crawled down his throat while he was asleep.

“It sounds like loads of banging and shouting. We should go and find the others. I’ll stay here, you should go and find them.” Insisted Chaffy. Broozer went to look for the rest of them. “Hi, we have found the hole. Chaffy’s guarding it.” Coughed Broozer.

“The police have returned and so have the demonstrators, it’s mad back there, we should keep low.” Gasped Flyer, who was just getting her breath back after running back from where the demonstrators were. She had sneaked there to check what the noise was all about. She was feeling rather tired and hungry and really just wanted to go back to her tent and sleep. All nine of them arrived back at the hole, where Chaffy was waiting. They quickly found where they thought the underground lake was and quickly planted two orchids.

“Right, only two more plants to go.” Smiled Flyer.

They decided to plant them near where they had found the large log.

"I'll phone THE RARE ORCHID SOCIETY again," suggested Prancer.

"It's only six o'clock in the morning, it's too early to phone, no one will be there," stated Scruffy.

"We should go back to camp for a couple of hours to have a sleep, shall we go back through the fields? I think we could be arrested if we go anywhere near the demonstrators," suggested Prancer.

Back at camp they found three policemen taking down their tents.

"What are you doing with our tents?" shouted Broozer.

One of the policemen said, "We're clearing out every demonstrator from this wood."

"But we're not demonstrators. We are from that village over there." Pointed Greg.

"Yer, we're on holiday," Broozer shouted again who was showing his anger. Flyer thought quickly.

"Yes, we all belong to a wildflower club." Lied Flyer.

"Even if you're not demonstrators, you still have to leave because there's a building project being started here," explained the second policeman.

"OK, we will go but can we leave in three hours just before the workmen get here?" asked Flyer.

"NO, YOU HAVE TO LEAVE NOW," shouted another policeman as they started to walk back into the wood.

"I'm going to ring THE RARE ORCHID SOCIETY to see if they are up yet. I have found if I climb up that tree I can get a really good signal," stated Prancer.

He had found a tree which was an easy climb because of his bad foot.

"Hello, hello, hello, are you on your way?" he asked.

"Yes, we're nearly at the wood. We started out at three this morning. We are so excited, we can't wait to see if you have found some Young's Helleborine. If you have, it will be a fantastic find," said the lady from the rare orchid society.

They took down their tents, put them into their rucksacks, and then walked towards the track. The Six Macs saw loads of black vans driving off into the distance with a couple of guards drinking smoothies. Greg decided to buy them all a smoothy while they waited, Scruffy asked for a cup of tea just in case his tooth started to hurt again.

"Hoot, hoot, hoot, peep, peep, peep." Two cars started driving towards them with a lady's arm waving from a little orange Mini. They stopped then jumped out.

"Hi, my name's Lyn. This is my assistant, Wendy. That's Phil and that's Neil."

"I'm pleased to meet you, I'm Flyer."

"We'll show you where they are," said Broozer.

They made their way towards the fence, Lyn showed her badge, the guard let her through.

"It just past that big oak tree," shouted Maltliquor.

Wendy knelt down with Phil, they were down examining the flower for about five minutes then jumped up.

"Yes, what a perfect specimen. You are right, their Young's Helleborine, are there any more?" asked Phil, who looked very official.

"We're not sure." Lied Broozer.

"Shall we all take a look further in the wood?" suggested Prancer.

The Six Macs led Lyn and her crew straight towards where the other two orchids were planted, which were above the Lake of Life.

"Look," shouted Neil.

They ran over to the other two orchids.

"WOW, we must look for more," shouted Lyn.

"Right, Neil and Wendy, you two go and look for the building manager to stop them digging. I'll take Phil to look for more, we'll slap a conservation order on this wood from now," stated Lyn in a stern voice.

"That's great, that means that the orchids won't be destroyed," said Prancer with concern.

"Yes, that's perfect, we are really happy we found the rare orchids before the workmen dug them up." Lied Broozer, who was pretending to be really concerned about saving the orchids.

"Yes, we're very pleased you found them as well." Smiled Lyn as she hammered a notice to the fence saying, CONSERVATION NOTICE Habitat of an Orchid called Young's Helleborine, anyone caught disturbing this habitat will be prosecuted. Lyn and the others thanked the Six Macs, then bought four fresh juices from Cafe Froot. Before climbing into their cars and driving off into the distance. As soon as they were out of sight, all Six Macs jumped high into the air.

"Yarhoooooo," they shouted.

"We did it, we actually did it, we've saved this wood, we've saved the Purple Orbs, we've saved the Lake of Life, can you believe it?" Laughed Flyer.

"It all happened so fast, I'm shocked, shocked with happiness." Smiled Prancer.

Flyer MacHigher raised her arm with a clenched fist the other joined her then all Six Macs shouted really loudly, "THE SIX MACS." David and Frank smiled. They all sat down, they were all totally exhausted, so decided to put their tents back up.

Maltliquor rushed back to Cafe Froot to buy more cans, he just caught them as they were packing up. It was not worth them being open now all the demonstrators and police had gone. Flyer was using Prancer's phone to text friends while sitting in a tree.

"I'm a bit worried about going asleep in case Jack enters my dream again, ain't you, Flyer?" asked Chaffy.

"Yes, me too, I don't want to ever end up down a hole ever again but she may just come back to thank us. Before I go to sleep, I'm going to write a poem about that beautiful lake, I want to remember it forever," smiled Flyer.

It was still the afternoon but the rest of them just wanted to sleep. Once their tents were up, they all crashed out.

Maltliqor was first to wake, then Flyer who was relieved that Jack had not entered her dreams. Suddenly Maltliquor shouted,

"Wow, come out, here." They all stuck their heads out of their tents, to their amazement the whole wood was covered in yellow primroses.

"Wow, it's Jack saying thank you," bellowed Flyer.

"Wow, I have never seen so many flowers, I believe your story about Jack now." Sniffled Trevor with a smile, his hay fever was always bad after a sleep.

"It's going to be dark soon and we have run out of food," complained Chaffy.

"ARRH HA, I have a surprise, look, what I have. I went to the smoothy bar to stock up that nice man gave me loads of cheese and ham wraps and some vegetarian ones with hummus in them. He said they will be stale by tomorrow. And I bought loads of tins of Coke Cola, so we can light a fire and have a party!" exclaimed Maltliquor MacSnigger.

“And I can play my guitar,” added Prancer. Flyer was still quite sleepy because she only slept for one hour.

“Before we party, does anyone want to hear the poem I wrote about the Lake of Life?” Flyer said nervously.

“Fire away.” Smiled David.

In Tranquillity,
I float,
In meditation,
Across a reflecting watery
Translucent purple forest,
Observing,
The power
of wondrous beauty,
With an emotion of content
deep in my heart.

“Wow that’s heavy,” said Frank. “Yes, it’s beautiful.” Smiled Trevor. “Yes, I think it’s really beautiful too, I just wish that I had seen it, I feel that I have missed out on something fantastically beautiful.” Smiled Prancer.

“But you without you Prancer this wood would have been lost. Let’s Party,” exclaimed Flyer.

The next morning there was a mesmerising pink sun rising over the hills in a distance. “I think before we go, we should hug the wise old oak tree,” suggested Flyer.

"Good idea." Agreed Chaffy.

Arriving at the oak tree they all held hands in a circle, surrounding the tree while leaning against it, then they closed their eyes. After a couple of minutes, they all felt the same feeling of happiness that floated through their bodies. It was a feeling of pure, pure happiness, they all smiled with a hunger for wanting to stay forever. Prancer suggests that they go but David and Frank wanted to stay just for another five minutes, so they did.

It was time to go. They strolled back to their camp, then dismantled their tents. It had started to rain really heavy, Prancer MacDancer dug a large hole, then they all helped to bury the burnt ambers from their fire. Before putting all their rubbish into bags, which they tied to their rucksacks. Leaving the area where they had camped back to how it was before, they had arrived. "There, I think Jack would be happy that," said Scruffy with a big smile.

"This is such a beautiful wood," added Flyer MacHigher. As she put a yellow primrose behind her ear, that she picked up from one of the thousands that covering the wood floor.

"That looks nice." Smiled Prancer.

"We will walk back with you as far as the river. We have decided to camp a few more nights there. Are you going back to your aunt's wood?" asked David.

"Yes, I think we're thinking of going straight back to my aunt and uncle's house, we're pretty wet and most of our clothes are really muddy," answered Scruffy MacTuffy.

They arrived at the tree which bridged across the raging river, then one by one they edged their way across.

On the other side they all exchanged phone numbers using Prancer phone. Then said goodbye as the Six Mac's walked away Trevor shouted,

"Thank you for the experience, we may see you next year." As they struggled, to put up their tents in the rain without getting their sleeping bags wet. "I liked them." Smiled Flyer, as she climbed a wooden stile.

"Cor, I'm rrreally tired. I need my nice ssssoft bed," stammered Chaffy MacTaffy who stammered even more when he was tired.

"I'm never going to cut a tree down ever again," stated Broozer MacDoozer.

"I'm not even going to break a twig," added Flyer.

Arriving at Chaffy's aunt's wood, the first thing they saw was a white fridge on its side with the door wide open. It looked like it had been dumped there and looked very unsightly. Maltliquor gave it a clean with one of his last coke cans and his last clean tee-shirt which left it a bit sticky. Flyer and Prancer went over to where the orchids were. They noticed a large pine tree had fallen right across them, hiding the places where Prancer had dug up the five orchids. All Six Macs walked slowly back to Bonnie and Bruce's house. Just before they arrived Chaffy raised his clenched fist, they all shouted, "THE SIX MACS."

They heard noises of people talking, so they went over to investigate, Daisy ran over to them jumping up Prancer's leg. "He knows you Prancer." Smiled Chaffy.

"Yes, she nearly got me caught when I was trying to dig up the orchids."

Prancer gave Daisy a pat on the head and said, "Sweet dog."

As they walked back towards the left-hand side of the wood, they spotted Bonnie and Bruce who was waving at them.

Bonnie shouted, "Do you want to help us? We have plenty of spades."

"What are you doing?" asked Chaffy.

"We're planting trees. The locals do this every year, it's fun."

"OOOw, I'm not sure, we're all soaking wet," answered Maltliquor.

"So are we," shouted Bonnie.

"Come on, more the merrier," shouted Bruce who was further away.

"Yes, come on, you lot, let's help, it will please Jack," suggested Flyer.

"All right pass the spades," replied Scruffy.

Prancer's foot was hurting a bit, so he sat in a hut next to a stable where a horse was sheltering from the rain. He started looking at what research had been done on trees, he found a really good article. Some professor had discovered that large fully grown trees, send extra water down their roots in areas where young saplings are growing to help them grow better.

Wow, now that's intelligent, he thought.

The End